CW00431752

We are all Falling Towards the Centre of the Earth

Collected Stories

by

Julie Travis

The Wapshott Press

We are all Falling Towards the Centre of the Earth

Published by

The Wapshott Press

The Wapshott Press
PO Box 31513
Los Angeles, CA 90031
www.WapshottPress.org

Copyright © 2017 Julie Travis

First printing June 2018

All rights reserved. Being works of fiction, any resemblance herein to persons living or dead is astonishing and purely coincidental. No part of this is publication may be reproduced or transmitted in any form or by any means, electronic or mechanical, including photocopy, recording, or any information storage and retrieval system now known or to be invented, without permission in writing from the publisher, except by a reviewer who wishes to quote brief passages in connection with a review written for inclusion in a magazine, newspaper, or broadcast.

ISBN: 978-1-942007-18-0

06 05 04 03 4 3 2 1

Wapshott Press logo by Molly Kiely

Cover image by Julie Travis

We are all Falling Towards the Centre of the Earth

Table of Contents

In memoriam Ian Johnstone (2.IX.67 – 30.VI.15).
Art Nature Magick Love

Foreword: (E)motion sickness

These stories have been written, for the most part, over a period of perhaps three or four years, although the concept of publishing them as a collection came about in Spring of 2016. Politically this was a turbulent time, a slow but deliberate car crash of a year, both here in Britain (my home) and later in the United States (the home of the Wapshott Press). This is a time when I would have loved two of my biggest influences—J G Ballard and George Orwell—to be here, to comment on the Black Hole that we've opened up, even if they couldn't keep us from being dragged into it.

Seeing the ultra-Right marching on the streets of Europe (including Britain, which has its most extreme Right-Wing government for many years) is something I always find shocking and shameful. Have we so easily forgotten the horrors of the recent past? We certainly seem determined to repeat them. Here in Britain, the wilful ignorance of so many has festered and become the absolute acceptance of hate crime. This is with the approval of a government happy to lay blame elsewhere for having made so many people's lives utterly miserable. Verbal and physical attacks on complete strangers, purely due to their difference to the attacker, have surged in recent years. There is a new generation of racists who want to think their politics are less odious because they call themselves 'alt' rather than 'ultra' Right, and who claim to be intellectual rather than thuggish, but it is just a rebranding of the same old bigotry.

However, it is not all bad news. Not everyone is fooled: political activism, a movement against such hatred, has become more visible, more mainstream, in recent times. In wildly optimistic moments I imagine this to be a sign of a 'waking up'; that people who've begun to question the current appalling state of their societies will realise that time is probably very short (the possibility of nuclear conflict has reared its ugly head again) and may wish to experience and participate in, rather than remotely viewing, their lives and the world around them. We have been seduced by technology into removing ourselves from the wonder of experience, we have happily become a society of spies and spectators and perhaps this has helped us to stop *seeing* our fellow humans — as people to communicate with, to understand and respect. Of course, when the bombs start dropping on us (as they constantly are in other parts of the world) life will be brought into brutal, hard focus. Will some insist on filming their own deaths in the ultimate narcissistic act ('selfie', after all, being an abbreviation for 'self-obsessed')?

Much of my writing is political in an abstract way, in the form of people with overpowering personal issues. It's not always obvious, but it's often politics that has got the protagonist into the situation they are in. Mental illness, for instance, can be a result of 'unconventional wiring' or a reaction to how certain people are treated by the world, its continuance partly due to the unavailability of effective treatment. The protagonists in my stories are on the outside of society, people who reject or are rejected by conventionality. They are generally survivors rather than victims, though, and most of them thrive on their singular way of looking at the world. It's how I identify and in whose company is my only hope of feeling comfortable. Perhaps, however, I should be more overtly political; I have no wish to be mistaken for a person who is happy with the way things are; the injustices of the human world, the enforced banality of ordinary life.

Another constant theme of my writing has been transformation; the potential to transform oneself — physically, spiritually, emotionally, psychically. But the stories in this collection were overwhelmingly driven by grief, dreams, isolation and death. After the last few years, which have been marked by terrible loss, I spend much of my time (in dreams and waking life) speculating and exploring what might happen to a person after physical death. For me, death is another form of transformation, a natural continuation of a soul's existence. My reading of female Surrealists/ Occultists in the last few years reflects this ongoing obsession; Leonora Carrington, Anna Kavan, Dion Fortune and Ithell Colquhoun are figures I feel a great connection with – to the point where it is as if I have, somehow, always been influenced by them.

The stories here are not cheerful tales, but nonetheless I don't see this collection as reflecting a completely bleak philosophy. We are far more than the fragile bodies we inhabit. If we disconnect from our determination to force the world, and nature, to adapt to our selfish demands, we may be able to reconnect with what humans are truly capable of.

My sincere thanks go to Ginger Mayerson and the Wapshott Press. Their belief in my work, over many years now, is greatly appreciated.

Julie Travis, Penzance, Spring 2018

We are all Falling Towards the Centre of the Earth

by
Julie Travis

Dark Fires

The starlings have gathered and begin their murmuration. They take the shape of a double-helix and fly past me in their formation. Once they've passed by, the murmuration breaks up and I am surrounded by the beating wings of a hundred thousand birds, before they turn east and head towards the rising sun.

The first time Maya died was the most frightening.

She wasn't dead for long, no more than a few minutes. Tending the plants on her kitchen windowsill, she became aware of an *aura*. She'd heard this happened as a prelude to an epileptic fit and tried to prepare for it. The flowers twisted and screamed in front of her and she dropped to the floor and nothingness. No arching muscle spasms, no pain, just *nothing*.

When Maya came to she knew that she'd been dead. How she knew was unclear but she was certain that her body had completely shut down and then re-started.

In shock, she managed to drink a glass of water, then cried, shaking so hard she knocked the glass off the table. For a while she felt horribly ill, her skin still corpse-cold and unresponsive, her body reluctant to do what she wanted it to. As the feeling began to pass, she wondered what the

1

cause of her temporary death had been. A stroke? A heart attack? Should she call an ambulance or see a doctor? Eventually it all felt unnecessary and she carried on with her day.

The second time Maya died was in public. Months had passed but she recognised the aura as soon as it appeared, a presence whirling around her. She was in a supermarket and tried to get to the toilets but dropped lifeless to the floor by the newspaper stand.

She awoke in an ambulance, the paramedic staring at her in shock.

"We've got her back!" he called over his shoulder to the driver. And then to Maya, "You decided to re-join the land of the living, then?"

How unprofessional, Maya thought, but was unable to say. The hospital carried out tests upon tests, the staff looking at her with a strange kind of suspicion, but no definite abnormality was found. When they decided to keep her in overnight for observation, she discharged herself. She knew she had died again and it was likely her test results were giving the doctors cause to suspect the same.

Given enough time, a person can get used to almost any situation, and over the next half dozen years Maya found that her frequent deaths became part of her life. There were adaptations to be made, of course; above all else she wanted her condition to remain private and under her control, as much as dying could be controlled. As she became less frightened by what was happening, she was able to detect the aura much sooner. It was almost nothing at first, a wisp of mist, heavy air that slowly materialised around her. It gave her time to go home and prepare; some water by her bed, curtains partly drawn. She could lay down in comfort and wait to die. But the auras were a blessing and a curse. To have warning of each imminent death helped keep it private but to know she was about to die—again—was torturous. Each death might be her last; she might not wake this time. To prepare for that possibility was impossible.

She began noting times, dates and the length of each period of death, trying to find a pattern. There was none, although she was concerned to see that the amount of time she was dead was increasing. What began as a few minutes became a few hours and, on the eve of her forty-first birthday, she remained dead for more than two days.

Once she was conscious and coherent, she became sick with fright; surely after fifty hours dead, her body would have begun to decompose? On the pretext of feeling run-down she made an appointment with her doctor. After her blood pressure and heartbeat had been checked and a blood sample taken, she went away with the advice to take a multivitamin supplement. It did not completely reassure her; her complexion was pallid and her eyes had a yellow tinge to them, but as the days wore on and her body functioned as normal, Maya began to relax. No real damage had been done. It was as if her body knew that each death was only temporary and reacted accordingly.

But if the effect on her body was minimal, the effect on her life was disastrous. Her social life became sparse, a love life impossible in such circumstances. Workmates thought her strange or a snob, assuming she thought herself above socialising with them. Closer friends knew that something was wrong, but no one was able to find out what it was. Some suspected mental illness and kept their distance.

The truth was so much stranger than their suspicions and Maya didn't know if she could ever put it into words. And death was becoming such an experience that little else seemed to matter in comparison. After the episode in the supermarket, where she could've been declared dead and woken up entombed in the hospital morgue, her fear of interference, of her condition being discovered, had clouded everything but once she was confident it would not be repeated, she was free to explore what was happening.

And death was not a blank space in her life.

A year after the episodes began; she became aware upon waking of what had happened while she had been dead. The memories were hazy, like an almost forgotten dream, but eventually it was undeniable that they were real experiences. By the time of her two day death, she had notebooks filled with memories of what happened when she died. At first she'd hovered above her body, recognising it but happily disconnected from it, like having thrown off wet, heavy clothes. Then the experiences changed as her spirit became more aware, more skilled with its freedom.

I am travelling, I am in Strange Places. I am surrounded by storm clouds, so fierce they're coloured red, so intense they're bursting into flame around me.

I am looking up at a million shooting stars filling the sky. I am travelling through Space at incredible speed.

These memories would come to her in flash-backs. They were exhilarating and nightmar-ish. Several times she collapsed in tears at work, which only added to the rumours about her men-tal health.

And then came the day the aura took her by surprise.

She was at work, taking notes at a meeting, listening to one of the participant's droning voice, when it changed. It became musical, beautiful. She looked up; the man's face was stretching, his jaw almost reaching the floor. And the air around her was heavy with mist.

Another death was almost upon her. How could she have missed it? Determined not to die in front of a roomful of people, she got up, meaning to head to the Sick Room, but instead lurched into the wall.

Navak, a woman she only vaguely knew, immediately saw that something was very wrong. She held Maya steady.

"Do you need an ambulance?" she asked.

Maya shook her head. "Sick Room," she managed to say.

Navak looked over her shoulder at the gawping faces. To their relief she said, "Carry on. I'll take care of her."

Maya was desperate to keep this latest death at bay until she was alone, but it swirled around her, seeping through her skin into her veins, muscles and bones, overtaking her. She was about to die. She gripped Navak's arm as the woman helped her onto the Sick Room's uncomfortable bed.

"Whatever happens," she said, "no ambulance, no one else. It's important."

I am climbing a silver ladder to the silver Moon. This is the path through Death. I am ecstatic and above me is the Moon, terrifyingly big. I am aware of my smallness here and revel in it. The size of Space is too much to take in. I am beyond the limits of comprehension, but I am glad to be here. I look down and see two Beings at the foot of the ladder. They are tall creatures, benevolent, following rather than chasing.

She returned to consciousness in tears. Navak had her phone in her hand, her finger hovering over the screen.

"You were gone. I could've sworn you were gone."

She had been giving Maya her inept version of CPR for several minutes and, despite her promise, was about to call for help.

"I'm fine. I will be fine," said Maya. There was nothing for it but to come clean. "I've been dying for years."

Navak drove her home and heard the whole bizarre story. Once she'd begun, Maya found it impossible to stop. To unburden such a load was irresistible. She broke down in tears, laughed, shouted, nearly screamed her tale. But she was also precise and provided such details that Navak had no choice but to believe her; after all, she'd seen Maya die and be resurrected before her eyes. She'd heard rumours about Maya being strange and unstable, and wished now that that was all the woman was. In reality her older colleague was carrying an unbearable weight. As she saw Maya into her flat she was made to promise not to tell anyone what had happened. To involve doctors and hospitals and tests was unthinkable.

"There's no cure for this. They'll have me embalmed and buried because they won't believe I'll come back. Please. This would kill my parents. You can't tell anyone."

And that potential horror was the only thing that could be worse than what Maya was going though. So Navak agreed, and Maya's extraordinary secret was safe. More than that, it was the beginning of Navak's life as Maya's confidante.

It was not a vocation Navak pursued. She did her best to forget what had happened but it was too monumental. Overnight it seemed that her life before this time had been reduced to nothing. Work, boozy weekends, her few brief relationships—all were time wasted. As the weeks passed she could not shake off the things she had seen and heard and so one Sunday Maya answered her door to find Navak standing there. They had not exchanged more than a few words since Maya had died in the Sick Room.

"I need answers. I need to understand what happened the other week."

Maya was not surprised to see her but was relieved that she was alone.

"The thing is, I need answers, too," Maya said as she poured wine for them both. "But over the years I've learnt to accept what happens, even to enjoy it. I just wish I had more control over it."

She could see Navak was floundering.

"It hasn't happened in the last few weeks. There's no pattern. At one point I thought there was. I was completely taken by surprise last time. I didn't intend for anyone to know about this. I'm grateful that you've kept it to yourself."

"How do you know that I have?"

"If you'd told anyone, they'd have been with you today."

It was true enough; who could keep away, knowing such a thing?

"How has this not driven you mad?" asked Navak. "To live with death constantly... it's unnatural. It's too much to deal with."

"Perhaps it's easier for me than it is for you. I can't imagine what it must be like to see someone die and then come back to life. And I have an awareness of my deaths, my experience of them is as real as this is now."

"I'm beginning to wonder if it's more real," Navak murmured.

She was full of questions that Maya couldn't answer and some that Maya didn't care to answer. These were things that Maya had spent years exploring; they were hers, knowledge acquired in places Navak had never been. She wanted to keep them to herself.

"The next time it happens," Navak continued, "the next time you know you're going to die—you can let me know if you want. I can keep an eye on you. If you don't want to keep dying alone."

Maya didn't hear her; the air was becoming visible. Such heaviness. Navak flattened and became two-dimensional. The only real thing in the world was the air, so Maya grasped a handful of it.

Navak guessed what was happening. Her first instinct was to run and leave Maya to her fate but she calmed herself, led Maya to her bedroom and lay her down. And was there to watch as death washed over her and dragged her under. It was peaceful, Maya the picture of calm, treading a now-familiar path.

Navak was not calm. She was terrified. What if Maya was dying for real, for ever? She ran to the kitchen and was sick in the sink.

Death lasted for eight days. Navak rushed to her side every evening after work. It was a hideous vigil; to all appearances Maya was dead. She neither moved nor breathed and her body was cold. Every day Navak nearly gave up, nearly called for an ambulance to make Maya's death official. Then she would gather herself and wash Maya down. In made for a sad ceremony. On the eighth evening she became aware of a glow around the lifeless body. It circled the bed, glowing in colours Navak had never seen before. It broke up and rained onto the figure on the bed. A little later Maya awoke and Navak realised she'd seen the woman's spirit re-entering her body.

I am on top of an angular stone structure, high in the mountains. From this point I look to one side and there is Saturn, close by, gigantic. The planet and its rings are glowing red. On the other side is a second Saturn. This one is made of silvery metal. Bizarre designs — hieroglyphs? Words? — are imprinted onto the planet's surface. What form do I take now, I wonder; I cast no shadow, I can see nothing of myself and as I move away from the mountain's edge, I approach another structure. It looks like a stone circle. As I get closer I see that it is made up of elaborate tombstones, the graves pointing inwards to the centre of the circle. On the far side of the circle stand three figures. Feeling my presence, they turn to me and I see their demonic faces. One begins to make its way towards me, around the outside of the circle. It will not step inside. They fade away as I Travel to another place. Surrounded by towering sand dunes, I see the two Beings again. They are walking across the sand, although they leave no trail. They walk slowly on bony legs with numerous joints. They are a long way away yet we are talking as if they are next to me.

"You are here, and yet you are not," they say. What had they been when they were alive—human, bird, mammal, plant, sea creature? Their form is reminiscent of all of these and none of them. Were they alive on Earth or some other planet? I sense that they are millions of years old. I explain that my deaths are temporary and not of my choosing.

"Beware the Abomination," they say. "Journey in company."

They disappear over the top of a sand dune and I am alone again.

Old habits die hard. It was Friday night and Navak was drunk. The pub was busy and Navak's group occupied a corner of it. One of them, Don, grabbed Navak as the music blared. She shook him off.

"What's wrong with you? You've been really weird lately," he yelled over the music. It was then that everything became clear to her.

"This isn't living," she spat. "I know dead people who live better than this."

And she walked out of the pub, more sober than she'd ever been in her life. Maya's long death had frightened her, ever more so as Maya refused to talk about her experience. What was she hiding? Once the worry was over, Navak had been furious.

"I watched over you for more than a week. Eight days, washing your cold body, convinced that you weren't coming back this time."

"You watched from the outside," said Maya. And then, a little spitefully, "That's nothing. It's my death, my experience. You haven't earned that knowledge."

"Have you any idea how pompous you sound? How selfish you're being?"

"No one asked you to be here. And you're being childish. This isn't a bag of sweets that I'm keeping to myself. I've spent years dealing with this on my own. I've almost lost my mind over it. And you think you can just share it with me?"

They hadn't spoken since, passing each other in the corridor at work with no more than a nod of acknowledgment. And now Navak was burning bridges with her friends. She had no regrets. It was pathetic to be living in such a way, without even the excuse of youth. Maya couldn't be so carefree. Navak envied the woman for her experiences although she couldn't imagine how horrific they were. Their lack of communication since their argument was depressing. She hoped Maya was as sorry as she was, but then again, what did Navak have to offer her?

When she got home from work that night, a parcel was waiting for her. Inside were several notebooks with a Post-It note stuck to the front of the first: "Read these. Every word. Then tell me if you're still interested in sharing what I'm going through."

So these were the secrets you've kept all these years, thought Navak. Alone in her bedsit, she spent the night reading the notebooks, at first in disbelief, almost laughing at one point but later reading silently, in awe. There were detailed descriptions of Maya's ordeal each time she died, which was bad enough, but Maya's experiences whilst dead were jaw-dropping. Were they hallucinations, dreams? People who had near-death experiences often spoke of amazing things, but these had been dismissed as visions created by chemicals in the brain. Maya clearly accepted them as genuine. They seemed to inspire her. And if they *were* real, how could Maya's life compare? Navak couldn't forget what she'd seen: *something* absorbed by Maya before she was resurrected. Science and religion would both react wildly to this. No wonder Maya wanted to keep this secret—between them they'd tear her apart.

"Who is the Abomination?" I ask the two Beings. I am hurtling through Space and they are beside me. They look at me but say nothing. I will have to find the answer myself.

They next met one lunchtime on a park bench near the office. Navak returned the diaries, a little reluctantly, knowing she would never read anything like them again.

"Death is changing me," said Maya quietly. "I've got papers to write and meetings to attend. It's all so irrelevant. I've already died again since we last spoke. I've just resigned from my job."

"What are you going to do now? You need your flat, your privacy."

Maya set her face, ready for the leap of faith she was about to take.

"I was hoping you'd take me in."

Navak smiled.

Maya's next death lasted for three hundred and sixty four days.

After selling nearly all her belongings, all the things most people held dear, she moved into Navak's bedsit. Six weeks later the aura descended again. Navak kept news of her new bedfellow secret, from her workmates and the friends who she'd more or less lost touch with anyway. She wrote to Maya's parents from Maya's email address to keep up the pretence that their daughter was well, but too busy to visit. It was not difficult. Her parents lived in the south of Spain and were not close to their daughter. It became normal to come home from work to Maya's lifeless body in her bed. At night she covered Maya in a blanket to prevent her coldness from keeping her awake. Whenever she felt her faith waning, she checked Maya over for signs of decay and, finding none, was satisfied.

During the ninth month, Navak was watching television when she heard noises behind her. She turned, expecting to see Maya conscious again but the woman was still lifeless.

The movement was next to her. Something was crawling from God knew where onto the air above the bed. It was an awkward shape with long legs, like a giant insect. As it pulled clear from wherever it was coming from it split in half. It was the two Beings. Navak recognised them from Maya's diaries.

They crawled across the air, fascinated by Maya's body. Navak sat still, hidden by shadows. She forced herself to breathe, even to ask a question.

"Where's Maya? I want her back."

Unsure whether she had spoken or just mouthed the words, the two Beings nevertheless ignored her while they peered at Maya. Eventually they acknowledged Navak but did not answer her question.

"Beware the Abomination," they said. They crawled into a crack in the air, hauling their limbs behind them, and were gone.

For the next three months Navak continued in her duties. It was a lonely task and she began to lose faith again, but one night she awoke and touched Maya's arm as she usually did, only this time there was a hint of warmth. Navak removed Maya's blanket and clasped her, ecstatic at the life beginning to flow through Maya's body again.

Recovery was much harder this time. A full twenty-four hours passed before Maya was coherent and could grasp how long she'd been dead. And when Navak described the appearance of the two Beings, Maya lost what little colour she had.

"What does it mean that they were here?" she asked.

"What does it mean that you were gone so long?" countered Navak. "Where have you been all this time?"

"I found *Harmonic Sanctuary*," said Maya. She didn't know what it meant or what it was, but she knew it was where she had been.

Piece by piece the dead year was coming back to her. This time had been different. In the past she had travelled to all kinds of places in and out of Space, to strange and otherworldly landscapes. Different planets, galaxies or planes of existence, she supposed. None had been the world she was alive in. But during her year's death she had repeatedly returned to a place she knew from childhood but couldn't quite remember; the shores of a lake. She had stood there over and over again in the last year—or however long that was in dead time—aware of the mountain that rose behind her. On one side of her was a tiny church, on the other a small wood. The water stretched out before her, like glass despite the cold wind blowing across the lake. And yet; something lay below the surface. What was it—the two Beings? The Abomination? Or just the memory of where this place was?

If that was the case, it broke the surface several days after she had returned to life. It was the day the two Beings crawled back into the world of the living.

Navak was on her way home from work, hopeful that Maya was there, alive, and had just crossed the road into her street when Maya came running towards her.

"The lake was in Cumbria!" she shouted. "I remember it. It's north of Keswick; the only natural lake in the Lake District. My parents kept telling me that." Navak, weary from the day, took a few moments to remember what Maya was referring to.

"Why would you go there, though?" she asked. "Of all the places on the planet, why there? Is it because it's a happy memory?"

Maya shrugged. "I have lots of happy memories," she said.

The air around her began to shimmer and Navak wondered if it was the aura descending again but Maya showed no sign of recognition. A fissure opened in the twilight and the two Beings slipped through. A dog, trotting ahead of its owner, barked at them then turned tail and ran back towards the comfort of its master.

Maya had discussed death with the two Beings at length. They had become familiar faces over the years, unlike the other creatures she met during death, who mostly passed by on their travels. She had talked to some of them but her repeated encounters with the two Beings had a calming effect and made her feel more comfortable with death. She thought that they were key to everything that was happening to her. It was clear they were trying to tell her something but were unwilling or unable to elaborate on what it was. Faced with them again, Navak was frightened and she, too, wondered what these creatures had once been. Not human, she was sure; there was a knowledge to them that was far beyond her species. Their skin was covered in lines, running like the rings of a tree around their limbs. Perhaps that way was the way to age them.

"Why are you here," asked Maya, "where I'm alive? Why have I been visiting a place that's on this planet?"

"The lake is where your boundaries between life and death are intertwined," said the two Beings. "Water is the pathway between the two worlds."

"Tell me what Harmonic Sanctuary is," said Maya.

"Musical notes can have a protective or a destructive effect," they said. "With the right notes and sounds we can build a Harmonic Sanctuary, that is, we can make a *hide* for you. It will be more difficult for the Abomination to find you."

"Why is it so important?" asked Navak. "Maya's safe while she's alive, isn't she? And if she knew what the Abomination was, she could avoid it."

The two Beings looked at her, their mouths opening wide and then closing so completely they disappeared.

"The next time will be the last," they said to Maya. "The Abomination crosses all worlds."

Maya had more questions but the two Beings silenced her. They were listening. The two women listened, too. All they could hear were normal, everyday sounds—the wind sighing through telephone lines, a blackbird's song, passing cars, a crying child. The two Beings gathered the sounds and began to construct something around Maya and Navak. Navak, protective as ever, went to push against it, but

Maya stopped her.

The Harmonic Sanctuary enclosed them both. It was as clear as glass but gave a distorted view of the outside world. The sounds of the world disappeared, replaced by the notes created by the Harmonic Sanctuary. The blackbird's song was there, but altered. The wind now sang through the telephone lines. It was all more beautiful than either of the women had ever heard. The Harmonic Sanctuary twisted and combined everything to create something new. It was majestic. Nothing in any world could touch them here, of that they were sure. The two Beings, however, could still be heard.

"We will take you to the lake," they said. Then, addressing Maya, "You must decide whether to continue your journey alone."

And Maya felt the aura making its way towards her, threatening to drown her for the last time.

Navak felt strangely at peace. The two Beings were benevolent; Maya was sure of it so Navak was reassured, although she felt less so as the street disappeared and was replaced by murkiness and the heaviness of water.

They were under the lake.

The water kept its distance, surrounding the Harmonic Sanctuary but not breaching it. The Sanctuary changed the sound of the water and of the fish and other creatures that lived there. The two Beings were just visible and beckoned them forward. Navak grasped Maya's hand and they stumbled a little before emerging onto the shores of Bassenthwaite Lake.

The barbed wire fence, covered in tufts of sheeps' wool that led out of the water; the marsh grass growing alongside the stream that ended its journey in the lake; the two hawthorn trees a few feet from the shore—Maya had only vague memories of this place but there was a beautiful familiarity about it. She squeezed Navak's hand.

"The aura's beginning to appear again," Maya said. "It's faint but it's there. I don't know how long I've got. If this is the last time, I need to learn as much as I can from the two Beings before I die."

"Won't the Harmonic Sanctuary protect you?" Navak was desperate. Nursing Maya's body through death was a lonely vocation, but infinitely preferable to freedom.

"I'm not sure I want it to," said Maya. "Everyone—and everything—dies. It's not a bad thing, it just *is*, I suppose. I've learnt that many different things exist after death. But each time I've died there's been something ominous on the horizon. Is it the Abomination? I need to know before I die for the last time. *That* will protect me."

They stayed by the lake for a week, sleeping on the shore, with the sounds of the Harmonic Sanctuary enhancing the area's beauty. Flocks of Canada geese moved constantly around the water, their wings beating silently as they took off and landed. Snowstorms blew across from the north, turning the landscape from green to white, covering the Sanctuary while they slept. The women awoke to nothingness, only to have the two Beings gently wipe the covering of snow away. And sometimes they moved to the strange music created by the Sanctuary.

Maya wanted to re-familiarise herself with the landscape, so they walked through the small woodland nearby and up towards the road that led to Keswick. On their return they headed to the tiny church that lay close to where they had emerged. Maya remembered a handmade bird box attached to one of the trees in the churchyard; devoid of birds, she had been delighted to find it contained the papery intricacy of a bees' nest. It would be long gone, of course, but she hoped the tree was still there.

But the little churchyard had been re-arranged.

The tombstones had been moved from their vague lines facing east, in order to make a gravestone circle.

Maya put her hands to her face.

"I've been to a place like this when I was dead, a long time ago," she said. "It's not the same place but the tombstones were like this." She stepped forward to confirm what she suspected. "With the graves facing inwards." She looked around her. "The place I went to had terrible creatures standing around it. Thank God they're not here."

What did it mean? Navak tried to remember what the two Beings had said—there had been something about the lake being where Maya's living and dead worlds met.

"I think everywhere you've been—ever—may be here somewhere," she said. Quietly she added, "This is where it all ends."

Maya heard her and nodded. "And I need to decide if I'm travelling alone."

She didn't phrase the next question. She didn't need to. If she was going to die in company, Navak was the obvious choice, although she was aware of how selfish it would be to ask such a thing.

The starlings that had begun to appear in the trees grew in numbers over the days and near the end of the week began to murmurate. Small groups flew in formation during the day, as if in practise and at dusk they joined together.

Maya knew what would happen.

In a massive gathering of a hundred thousand birds, the starlings swept around the women in a beautiful cloud, then re-formed as a gigantic double-helix. They took up the sky with the shape, making it roll and turn. Then it positioned itself over the yew trees that surrounded the church and broke apart as the starlings dropped into the branches to roost.

The women tried to talk but couldn't be heard above the excited chatter of the birds. The two Beings, too, seemed overwhelmed by what they had seen.

"In the morning the birds will fly towards the rising sun," they informed Maya. "That is when you'll die for the last time. You must decide tonight if you'll be alone."

"Tell her what the Abomination is!" said Navak. "How can she decide anything without knowing that?"

The two Beings ran their hands over the Harmonic Sanctuary, checking that all was well with its construction. Their voices came through, a little faded but more melodious than before.

"You know what the Abomination is," they

told Maya.

She thought carefully. All the places she had been to during death had one thing in common—the storm-clouds looming on the horizon. More distant than some of the dangers she had faced, she had all but overlooked them. They were not storm-clouds, she realised now. It was an atmosphere, a feeling; something that could engulf her, wrap itself around her and never leave.

The Abomination was hopelessness. And in death it would be disastrous; oblivion, forever. She looked up at the two Beings. "If I'm alone, I'm more likely to find hopelessness. That's what the Abomination is; losing belief in where I am."

They lay beside Bassenthwaite Lake that night. Despite the Harmonic Sanctuary, Maya could feel the grass beneath her, could smell the earth. The music of the Harmonic Sanctuary accompanied her. She was glad—she wanted to experience as much as she could and the simplest things, the things she had so often taken for granted, were more beautiful, more heady than she'd ever known. There was no time left for hesitation. She asked Navak if she would join her on the journey. She took care not to plead.

Navak knew the question was coming, had suspected it for some time. It was only logical for Maya to ask her it. Her initial feeling was to accept; the worlds that Maya had described were fantastic. To travel them with her would be beyond anything she could have imagined death to be.

But in that lay a problem.

Her reason for having helped Maya all this time—devoted herself to the woman—was that her own life had little meaning. Her thirty-six years of existence had been without direction. Was it right to die without having really lived? She knew now that death wasn't the end of things. It was liberating.

"I've thought about this for a while now," she said. "And part of me really wants to come with you. But I can't. I need to live first."

Maya closed her eyes. "Of course. I understand. I may not have a choice, but you do."

"But you can't go alone," said Navak, anxious again. "It's nearly sunrise. There's no one else here to ask."

Maya smiled. "Yes, there is."

The two Beings were in the woodland watching the starlings sleep. They turned at the sound of the Harmonic Sanctuary's approach and nodded when Maya asked if she could join them on their travels.

"You need to learn from this life before you proceed to the next," they said to Navak.

They took down one side of the Harmonic Sanctuary to let Navak out, then rebuilt it around Maya, who was delighted to find the sounds changing as the shape of the Sanctuary changed. The four of them made their way down to the edge of Bassenthwaite Lake. Maya was finding it increasingly difficult to walk. The aura had been around her for some time now, creeping around her body. Death was close.

Navak, anxious at the prospect of being so

close to the end, was again tempted to join Maya, so much so that she took a step forward when the others stood on the shore, and it took all her courage to stop again.

The two Beings spoke to her one last time. "You must still help Maya," they said. "You will make your way home from here. Maya's body will be there. It must be cremated. Then you will both be free."

Navak wasn't sure she wanted to be free, but the decision had been made, and it was heartening to know that she still had a part to play. The three of them began to walk into the lake. Maya, just visible in the half-light, looked different from outside the Harmonic Sanctuary. Slightly distorted, her expression was nevertheless clear and calm. She looked back only once. Neither of the women spoke. The words to express what was happening had not been invented.

Navak watched until they were under water, until the last ripple had made its way to the shore. As the sun rose she heard a great cacophony; the beating of wings and high-pitched chatter as a hundred thousand starlings took to the sky and flew east.

Maya, then, was dead.

Feeling vulnerable without the protection of the Harmonic Sanctuary, and now alone in the world, she bathed in the lake, baptising her new life.

It was time to make plans. After she had made her way back to London and said her private goodbyes to Maya, she would arrange her cremation and tidy up what little of her affairs remained. Then she would visit Maya's parents in Spain with one of her friend's few remaining possessions to give them, and the diaries for herself. After that—who knew? Maya had said that she was consumed by death, over and over again. Navak wanted to be consumed by life before death caught up with her. And if she was lucky, when that happened she would find Maya again.

I am surrounded by stars; a belt of them on either side, stretching to eternity. The two Beings and I have been drawn here. Two galaxies are in the process of colliding, they tell me. We are traversing the ever-narrowing gap between them. The pressure is crushing me but we are at the birth of something new, the formation of a super-galaxy. The stars, the planets, the spaces between them are all alive in their own ways. Just as I am alive even though I have died.

Beautiful Silver Spacesuits

Sometimes the only way to tell a story is from the end.

My story, then, began with my best friend Remaine in the throes of death, but a death like no one has ever seen. She stood before me, shivering, her flesh turning grey. Then she died, one inch at a time. And the most horrific thing about it was that I had never seen her so happy.

"I am all the stars in your galaxy. All the stars of the Universe," she said. "I am all the elements which surround us."

What did it mean? What was she talking about?

This odd behaviour had only begun in the last few weeks. Remaine had always been straight talking, so the fact that she'd started speaking in riddles was baffling. I asked her, as I had half a dozen times before, what she meant.

She looked haunted. Hunted. It made me glad she was safe, at my place. Then she muttered something and was back to her usual self, with no memory of what she'd just said. And she was tired. She'd had another long day at work. No doubt that was all there was to it.

"Are you still in the shop on your own?"

Remaine nodded. "Nearly all the time. Josephine pops in."

"Because she doesn't trust you; she doesn't do any work."

"She's got to keep everything going while her brother's ill. She does a bit of paperwork, gives me a proper lunch break sometimes. And she's looking after Zedd. He's not going to be away from his precious shop for longer than he has to be."

I drank some wine. It was better than making the comment that came to mind; that Remaine was being taken advantage of.

I had a day off during the week, so I went to see Remaine at work. I hadn't been there for a while and I stood inside the door, taking in the atmosphere. Behind the small shopfront lay a treasure trove. The smell gave away the shop's purpose before one even laid eyes on the rows and rows of books that lined the walls.

Remaine was Assistant Manager of Reverie, my favourite second-hand bookshop. The building was one of the oldest in town, long and narrow, but wide enough to be able to browse in without getting in anyone's way. At the back were two sofas; people were welcome to try before they bought. A staircase behind them led to the basement, which housed the fiction and had a small space for readings. The shelves and décor were dark, but it looked sophisticated rather than dingy. Birdsong played over the speakers, just loud enough to be relaxing. And the smell! A combination of mustiness and old leather bindings. Some of the books had clearly been stored in lofts or garages, perhaps forgotten for years before being unearthed and brought to the shop. I favoured the ones that had clearly been read many times, the much loved but well-kept volumes. I flicked through a couple of these, imagining who had read them over the years, how difficult the decision might have been to part with them, or whether the owner had died and those left behind had had to clear a house without having enough time to discover what treasures were there. No wonder Remaine didn't complain about the long hours. This, after all, was her dream job.

Of the two floors, I preferred the ground floor, with its eccentric reference books, everything from early metro maps to the Occult to parasites of the rainforest. Truth had always been more strange and wonderful than fiction. I resisted the temptation to browse for longer. Remaine would be downstairs. I stopped on the first step at the sound of raised voices.

There was an argument going on down there, involving several people by the sound of it. Harsh words were being spoken, male and female voices cutting across one another. I couldn't hear Remaine's voice, but if she was down there she might need help. I clattered down the stairs—I didn't want to surprise anyone who was already agitated.

The basement was empty. Silent.

I couldn't see the whole floor from there. A tiny office lay at the far end, next to the space used for readings and performances, but it wasn't big enough for more than two people. From it Remaine emerged, duster in hand. She smiled at me, not questioning why I was looking in every corner to see where the other people were hiding. It chilled me to the bone to find no one there.

We went upstairs and talked for a while. Everything was normal. She was normal. Remaine had no knowledge of an argument taking place and laughed when I told her I'd heard voices.

"It's been really quiet all morning," she said. "Either we have ghosts here, which I'm not aware of, or you're... " and she tapped her temple. She laughed again. It was a hollow sound. I didn't join in.

That night I dreamt about the argument. There had been three male voices and two female voices, I was sure of that. The argument was replayed word for word. It was furious, but nonsensical. Each person had their own agenda which had nothing to do with what anyone else was saying. I woke up. It had been like listening to four lunatics raving. But there had been only one person in the basement. And since I don't believe in ghosts I could only conclude that, unknown to Remaine, she had provided the voice to all of those people.

All this was happening in the shadow of The Bomb, something that hadn't fallen across us for thirty years. Back then I had thought it inevitable that Europe would be the arena for a nuclear war. Too young to understand the politics, I'd had nightmares and anxiety attacks over the impending end of the world. And now that fear had returned. The decades of knowledge in between just made me more aware of why the situation was so precarious. Could this be behind Remaine's recent strangeness? Exhaustion and fear, long periods alone in the shop; was her argument with herself a sign of depression?

Fear was evident all around me. I had observed some absurd behaviour on the high street—two businessmen handing out money and confidential files, a woman walking naked with the words *I am Atomic—touch me and die*, written on her torso in lipstick. Cracks were beginning to appear. It frightened me to think Remaine could be in similar mental distress.

My own fears were manifesting in day and night dreams. My childhood obsession with Space had never really left me, despite the derision of my family and teachers, but now it was stronger than ever. I found myself there more and more, an astronaut blasted into Space to dock with the International Space Station. Everything that happened there took time. Endless patience, working in slow motion, a super-awareness of everything around me—all were necessary in my dream-work. Perhaps it was just my way of meditating, of keeping panic at bay. And so maybe Remaine was simply adopting her own coping strategy but I was worried about the long term effect it might have on her. I wanted to talk about what was happening—to the world and to her—but I didn't know how to start such a conversation. Eventually it was Remaine who began talking about the build-up to war and how much it scared her.

"I was born just after the Cuban missile crisis," she said. "I don't remember it, but my parents must have talked about it. There were echoes of anxiety all around the house."

My own parents hadn't talked about it, or the nuclear threat of the 1980s, but I was aware of it hanging over us via newspapers and the anarchist punk records I bought. But that gave me an outlet, people to share my fears with. Remaine had been more isolated and cut off from any discussion or support.

"It all seemed so preordained. And now here we are again in the same situation," she said. And then she whispered calmly, "I've been expecting the end of the world since the day I was born."

I was learning new things about her. I'd known she was a member of the Campaign for Nuclear Disarmament and other political groups at various times, but I didn't realise she'd spent her whole life afraid. I wanted to ask about the incident in the bookshop, to tell her I was worried about her, but she seemed so low that I held back. I was her friend; it was my responsibility to keep an eye on her.

This time the dream, which I had during the day time, when I was supposed to be working, progressed, and I was outside the International Space Station on a Spacewalk. I was above the Earth and I looked down at the clouds and oceans and I knew that no one who saw the planet like this could start a war that would destroy it so utterly.

Remaine was beginning to shrink. The essence of her was becoming smaller, harder to find. The other voices that had begun to show themselves were taking hold.

And there were so many of them.

The things that I was worried might be wrong with her—stress, depression, nervous exhaustion—paled when I realised what she must really be suffering from. *Multiple personality disorder* was a frightening term and I was desperate to learn what it might mean before facing her with it. I tried to be rational about it but much of the time it seemed to me that she'd been possessed. The situation in which we found ourselves, the prospect not only of death, but the destruction of our beautiful world was so terrifying that it was as if it had already begun before a single missile had been fired. The only hope Remaine had was in her job. Despite her being taken advantage of by Zedd's sister, and perhaps by Zedd himself, Reverie might be the only place where Remaine would be, and feel, safe. The outside world was more unstable by the day. People's terror manifested itself in increasingly destructive behaviour. Deliberate motorway pile-ups, uninhibited behaviour in public, groups gathering to self-harm—chaos was on the increase.

The bookshop was beginning to suffer due to Remaine's strange outbursts. Each customer was being served by a different part of her fragmenting personality. I'd gone to the shop to see how Remaine was and had observed one customer being treated subserviently—which Remaine would never have done—while the next was bombarded with manic chatter about nothing to do with the book she was buying. No one had complained yet but word was spreading and sales fell as people became wary of entering the shop. In her lucid moments Remaine was aware that something was wrong. Most of her regulars had stopped visiting and she was upset.

"Do you think it's all the talk of war that's doing this?" she asked me one day. "Do people just have other things to think about?"

I shook my head. "We need more of an escape than ever. What better way than with books?"

I told her my own method then. It was the first time I'd shared it with anyone since my childhood ambition had been dismissed. It was a way in to talking about Remaine's condition.

"I'm not sure how much control I have over these thoughts now," I said. "It's more than a day dream. It's so real that it's difficult to concentrate on everyday things. What about you? You haven't seemed yourself lately."

Remaine's expression became sad and confused.

"I'm forgetting things and having blackouts. I know I've been working a lot but I don't remember much of it. Yesterday I was suddenly aware of being in Reverie but I don't know how I got there or what I'd been doing all day."

After some prompting, she agreed to see her doctor. She waited on the phone for twenty minutes then had a short conversation with the receptionist and hung up.

"There's so much demand for appointments that I won't be seen for weeks. She wouldn't even book me in, just told me to keep calling back in case there's a cancellation."

She looked worse now than I'd ever seen her. And fragile; something I'd never known her to be. I felt bad for convincing her she needed help that was impossible to get. I told her that she could talk to me about anything. After a pause, she spoke.

"I'm lonely," she said. "But everyone is these days. Fear isolates you."

She put her head in her hands and I saw a mark on her neck. It looked like dried blood, so I asked her if she'd had an accident. She didn't remember, so I took a closer look and was dumbfounded to find a tattoo on her neck; the letters "r n c" in blood-red ink. The tattoo looked old, but was in good condition and written in beautiful script.

"When did you get this done? I've not seen it before. What does it mean?"

Remaine was almost angry now, insisting she'd never had a tattoo. She looked at it using a pair of mirrors.

She stared at it for an hour, then looked at her own reflection as if it was that of a stranger.

Later, when she was herself again, we went to a café. I hoped it would buoy us both to be out. The news, as ever, interrupted the background music. I tried not to listen, but certain phrases were impossible not to hear; *pre-emptive strike, mutually assured destruction.* I looked around the café—the spectre of the past had fallen across everyone, even the young. I tried to smile.

"This is why people need books," I said. "We all need to escape from this."

But Remaine had disappeared and was someone else again. I wondered if it would be wrong to envy her.

~

That night; a nightmare. The Spacewalk was wonderful. I raised my arm and the Sun reflected off the silver material. I am made of silver, I thought. I am beautiful. And in the low gravity my metal body was weightless. Looking down at the Earth, I was moved to tears. I could see Africa, the great continent surrounded by blue. But then part of the landmass was obscured. A flash of light followed by a mushroom cloud; the unmistakable sign of the detonation of an atomic bomb. The suicide of the human race had begun.

The radio alarm woke me with the news that, amid *escalating tensions*, people were attempting to leave major cities in droves. I rang Remaine. There was little chance that our unimportant town would be targeted by a nuclear bomb but that was almost irrelevant; after all, did we even want to survive such a war?

Remaine was in no fit state to work — several people raved at me from her end of the line. I told her I'd ring Zedd if she would give me his number, but Remaine's personas were constantly changing. It was exhausting just listening to them all. I gave up and put the phone down.

During my lunchbreak I hurried to the bookshop. I found Remaine lying on the basement floor, trying to pick up the books scattered around her. I went upstairs to shut the shop and was relieved to find Zedd's sister, Josephine, walking through the door. I explained the situation — a version of it, anyway.

"This is not the first time she's been taken ill recently," she said, clearly irritated.

Remaine was herself only fleetingly while I

got her out of the shop. She laughed at Josephine and accused her of being a Jezebel. Except it wasn't Remaine, it was an elderly man with an American accent. Josephine looked disgusted. I could only apologise on Remaine's behalf.

I stayed with Remaine for the next two days; she was incapable of being left alone. She was furious with me for interfering, then begged me in a dozen different voices to let her go to work. All her personas were as one about this. It was bizarre to suddenly hear those voices demanding the same thing rather than being engaged in their personal monologues. I was tempted to let her go—it might be calming for her to be there—but I was too worried and frightened. I should have rung her doctor. Remaine urgently needed to see a psychiatrist but I hung back, not wanting to take such a step without her consent.

On the second night we sat up until very late. I did my best to talk to my friend, but every answer came from a different person. Each made sense in itself, but became gibberish when put with anything else. Over the weeks I'd tried to compile a list of her separate personalities to see if there was a pattern of some kind—if there were voices she used more than others, and in which situation—but, as far as I could tell, no personality was ever repeated. I stopped when the list reached three figures. Similarly, I'd tried to name them, to make them less frightening; Rocket Woman, Mr Ghost, The Architect, The Golden Sea Captain—had these personas returned, they would have had a reassuring familiarity, but each made only a single visit.

While she spoke, Remaine stood at her bookcase, running her hand lovingly over the books, picking one out and feeling the air on her face as she flicked through it. I continued talking, needing to maintain some sanity in the room. I told Remaine about my dreams, how symbolic they were and how euphoric it felt to be removed from the planet and all the danger we were in. She put the book down and turned to me.

"I don't want to be here anymore," she said, as herself now.

It was the saddest thing I'd ever heard. Perhaps she knew how ill she was, that she would likely lose her wonderful job soon and that the world might be changed in devastating ways. It was as if Remaine had managed to get her head above water, before being dragged under, perhaps for good this time. And I decided then, just before I fell asleep, that we both needed help with her condition. I would demand an appointment with the doctor if necessary.

My dream began from the beginning. I heard the countdown, blasted off into Space, docked with the International Space Station and prepared myself for a Spacewalk.

I felt free on the outside of the Station. Looking around, I realised I had no safety harness— I was attached only by my magnetic boots. The Earth was below, the Sun rising, revealing South America and then—mushroom clouds. The Andes, the Western spine of the continent, was being obliterated. There were no cities nearby. It was destruction for its own sake. Inside my helmet I sobbed and the vision blurred before clearing again. I closed my hands slowly around the rail above me and pulled my feet free of the Station. I let go and pushed away, away from the Earth.

The Sun reflected off my silver spacesuit, blinding me at times, but making me feel as if I was made from the precious metal again. So polished and clean, I must have been visible for hundreds of light years. The light began to dim as I moved away from the Sun. It didn't frighten me. Moving in Space was liberating. Where was I going? I knew I'd be in darkness for a long time, but eventually I'd be far enough away from home to reflect the light of another star.

What did Remaine dream of? Was she herself then, the other personas silenced for a time? Or was she split into even more fragments, when all her defences were down? All this time I'd been her friend and yet I hadn't realised how lonely she was, how frightened — not just now, but all the time I'd known her and beyond, throughout her life. I'd failed her.

And what of that tattoo? Why go to the trouble to get a few random letters tattooed onto her neck and then hide them? It was possible, though, that Remaine had no previous knowledge of it. Who knew which of her other identities had been in control when it was done?

I woke up after a few hours' sleep to find the flat empty. Remaine had left the radio on, tuned in to a news station. It was endlessly analysing the stand-off in the Sea of Japan, with a political commentator declaring the Doomsday Clock now stood at a few seconds to midnight. I felt panic closing in around me and switched the radio off. I could imagine Remaine listening to those relentless reports; already scared, she'd run from them.

But where to?

The bookshop was the only place I could think of. It was her refuge, full of birdsong and all the stories—all the escape—she could ever wish for.

Reverie was busy when I got there. One person was by the till, trying to buy a book.

The others, a dozen or so, were listening.

Above the sound of a cuckoo's call playing over the speakers was the sound of voices. It was as if the basement was full of people. It had to be Remaine.

When I got down the stairs Remaine was in the middle of the room, books piled up in her arms. She embraced them as she spoke, screamed, shouted each sentence in a different voice, her expression and posture continually changing. As footsteps calmly trod the staircase behind me, Remaine dropped the books and glared with malevolence at the person standing behind me.

"I told her she was sacked," came Josephine's cold-hearted voice. "We had complaints. And no wonder."

I ignored her. Remaine was all I cared about. She was still in there somewhere. She cursed Josephine with the voice of a child. And then she began to die.

Remaine shivered uncontrollably, goose pimples breaking out on her arms. Her olive skin that had always been so beautiful turned grey. Every drop of moisture in her body was evaporating. A layer of skin fell from her forearm. As it touched the floor it became powder, whirling around as if a great wind were whistling around the basement. It circled for a while and then, glinting in the sunlight that streamed in from the window, headed purposefully towards a section of the fiction.

It was not powder, but dust.

As the dust moved amongst the books, filing itself away in the appropriate place, I at last realised what had happened to Remaine. She'd spent so much time here, caring for the books, captivated by them, that she had absorbed them. The dust from all the pages of all the books that had ever passed through the shop had found a loving home. Remaine had soaked up all the stories and characters until she was overflowing with them. And now, with the fear of war hanging over us all, she was falling apart. But she was not dying. She was returning. She turned her head and I got a final glimpse of the text on her neck. It was from a novel, then; not a tattoo but part of a word she hadn't fully absorbed.

Remaine was escaping from a world that was now unbearable, becoming part of a thousand fantastic tales. As each inch of her turned to dust I knew she was finally safe, but I was losing my best friend and despite the joyful smile that broke out on her face I wailed with grief. And I willed myself to dream my dream again, only next time it would need to be endless so I, too, could escape and would be floating, forever, through Space.

The Spoiler

"And that," said the Spoiler, "is what happens in the end."

The boy looked up at her as he chewed on his tobacco.

"You die young," she continued. "But not of cancer, surprisingly enough." The Spoiler smiled. It was not reassuring. "The woman who will by then be your wife will not be by your side. She'll barely notice you've gone."

The boy spat his tobacco out, close enough to the Spoiler to appear defiant.

"Damn you! I don't care," he said, with all the bravado a fifteen-year-old possesses. But tears ran down his face as he walked away.

The Spoiler had been alive for many lifetimes. Those who found life a great adventure were left with a bitter taste in their mouths once the Spoiler had been to visit and those who found life a bitter experience had all their cynicism confirmed.

"To be told a story's ending when one is still on the first page is to have one's hopes truly dashed," was the Spoiler's favourite saying. It never failed to make her smile.

Rosa Rugosa first dreamt of the Spoiler when she was seven years old, and continued to dream about her throughout her childhood. How she knew the woman's name was something she could never remember; it was just there, hanging in the air like a ghost.

The Spoiler was an uninvited guest. At first all Rosa really noticed was the woman's appearance. Her blue hair was short, like a boy's, and she dressed in a way that Rosa's mother disapproved of—a vest top, despite her size, and camouflage trousers. Rosa's mother was always trying to be thin and thought fat women should either stay indoors or cover themselves up. The Spoiler did neither.

Her clothing not only revealed her flesh, but the thick lines tattooed over her body. Blood-red, they made a big 'Y' on her belly and forked in the middle of her chest, the lines running over both sides of her collarbone before stopping on top of her shoulders. There was another red line on her head, running across her forehead and around, like a permanent hairband. It was just visible amongst her spikes of hair. Rosa thought the tattoos lovely.

The woman, however, was not. For many years she didn't speak, not properly. Rosa heard voices, sometimes slowed down, sometimes whispered, sometimes shouted in her ear. She knew it was the woman's voice and she knew the woman was called the Spoiler, which was a funny name. Other things she said didn't sound human. To Rosa it sounded like the chattering of birds.

When Rosa bled for the first time, she had her last dream about the Spoiler. This time she understood what the woman was saying. The

Spoiler's eyes lit up as the thin trickle made its way down the inside of her thigh.

"Much more blood to come," she said, delighted.

Rosa repeated this to her parents. It was an unguarded moment, brought about by menstrual cramps and the fear of enforced growing up. Her father turned away, embarrassed. Her mother grabbed her and asked her what the Devil she meant, a turn of phrase that was not lost on Rosa.

"It's what the Spoiler told me," she blurted out.

Her mother didn't hear, or chose not to hear what she'd said. Rosa was alone. It was a moment, she realised, that would define her life.

She watched as he opened his front door, with the same nonchalance he opened it every day, but she knew that this day was different and soon he would know it, too.

The one thing that was out of place in his world was the bloody knife that sat on his doorstep, so his eyes were drawn to it.

He made to pick it up and stopped. He looked around, his eyes wide open, hoping not to see the maniac he imagined.

Best to put him out of his misery. The Spoiler stepped into view and picked up the knife.

"You can't touch that! The cops will need it for evidence," said the man.

The Spoiler winced. She'd never liked a Texan drawl.

"They won't," said the Spoiler, "the knife doesn't exist yet."

Enjoying the man's confusion, the Spoiler continued. "It hasn't been manufactured yet. It will spend some years in a kitchen drawer a few streets away from here. And this is what it'll look like in eleven years' time, when it's been used to cut your throat with."

He was gawping at her; *she* was the maniac.

The Spoiler held up her free hand. "Not by me. I don't kill people. I just bring *tidings*. Shall I tell you who does kill you?"

It wasn't really a question; of course she was going to tell him.

He slammed the door shut.

The Spoiler made her way towards the back of the house.

Rosa almost forgot about the Spoiler. There was a year when she drifted and almost became an ordinary 12 year old girl, but when she was online one day she typed 'the Spoiler' into the search engine before she realised what she was doing. Amongst the sites thrown up—film and comic and gossip sites—a folklore site caught her eye. When she viewed it, its appearance was so unsophisticated that she nearly didn't bother to read it. But it did contain a reference to the Spoiler. How was it possible that someone from her childhood nightmares was based on an obscure figure from folklore? As Rosa read on, she found the Spoiler was said to have existed in most of the countries of the world over the last few centuries and had last been heard of in England in the early 1940s. She changed her appearance from country to country and time to time, presumably to blend in a little more, but her mission — one she seemed to relish, it was noted — remained the same.

The Spoiler, too, had long been aware of crossing Rosa Rugosa's path. She did not usually bother analysing dreams — after all, there was only a certain amount of Time, even for her — but these were different. They felt *physical*, as if she was being dragged in and out of Rosa's head. It took her far away from where she was travelling or carrying out her duties but it made her think about England and how she must return. Her last stay there had been during the Second World War, a busy and therefore happy time for her. To face so many people and tell them, in great detail, how their stories would end had been enchanting. Beyond their disbelieving expressions was the look in their eyes that knew this was no tasteless prank. The eyes always dimmed then and the Spoiler knew the light that had shined there would never return.

Everything was different in Rosa's dreams. Here communication was difficult. Was it the state of dreaming or Rosa herself who made it so? The girl was unfamiliar with the language, which was strange — perhaps she wasn't aware that she was dreaming. Gradually the Spoiler gained control and began to remove herself from them.

But she never completely disappeared from Rosa's thoughts. She Skyped the authors of Forgotten Folklore, the site that had given her a taste of the Spoiler's history. They were an old gay couple (in their early 50's but to a 13 year old they were ready for the grave), two men who had spent most of their lives researching obscure pieces of folklore. Claiming to be working on a school project, she asked for their sources, sorely lacking on their scrappy website. In reply, their laptop was picked up and carried through to a small room lined with books.

"We've got books and pamphlets that probably had a run of two or three hundred, way back when. Most of which would've been destroyed, either by accident or design. This really is forgotten folklore," said a voice in the background before the laptop settled onto another table and Giovanni's face returned to the camera. "So, what's your interest in the Spoiler?"

He had a strong accent. It took Rosa a minute to understand what he was saying, then she spoke quickly.

"I'm not especially interested in her," she said. She was not ready to talk about the dreams, about what the Spoiler had said to her.

"Wise not to be," he replied. "Our studies show folklore to be a mixture of half-truths, memories and imagination... "

"Except in a few cases, and the Spoiler's one of them," said Peter, suddenly coming into view. "We found many of the stories about her — from whatever country over the last four hundred years or so — so consistent that they sounded like the history of a real person. Or several. She's been in England in living memory — just — yet we couldn't find anyone who would talk about her. We knew they could, because the evidence pointed to them or their parents or grandparents having actually met her."

"Why wouldn't they talk?" said Rosa. "From what I know, people like passing these stories on. It sounds as if they really believed in her."

"More than that," said Giovanni. "It was as if they knew her to be real. And they were afraid."

"I know the forbidden can be very attractive," said Peter. "But this is best left alone."

"Devil, Devil, I defy thee!" the woman hissed.

Such flattery. The Spoiler ran her fingers through her blue hair, pouting like a glamour model.

"I'm not the Devil, I'm just a biographer," she said. "I've given you the minutiae of the rest of your life. Just think! You've spent thirty-two years in utter ignorance. Exactly half your life. What kind of existence is that? You now know how the second half will be. I'll never know why people aren't grateful."

Dread was threatening to choke the woman.

"I'll change that story!" she hissed, her teeth gritted so tightly that she was barely audible. "I'll kill myself. You won't win, you fat bitch!"

The Spoiler cupped her hand to her ear, smiling at the threat and what the woman regarded as an insult.

"It's not about winning," she said. "I don't create your life story. But I can see that you hoped for something else, something *more*, perhaps, than banality. What you wish, however, is impossible; you cannot alter a sculpture once it's been cast."

The Spoiler turned around to admire the view. Holy Island was one of her favourite places. She loved the way the rock rose from the little island, how the castle perched on top of it, the architect's pitiful attempt to reach Heaven.

It was good to be back in England.

Giovanni and Peter had managed to warn Rosa off pursuing the Spoiler. For a while, anyway. Fascinated by their obsession, she began to contact them on a regular basis. They talked about folklore, hauntings, the desire to believe in something outside of normal existence.

"Are we just fooling ourselves?" Giovanni asked her more than once. Rosa's earnest face peered back at him from the computer screen. She would shake her head, aware that he was teasing her, but unable to resist taking the bait.

"There's too much evidence! All of that stuff in your library! If only a fraction of it is credible, then it's enough."

They loved her enthusiasm, her analytical mind. It helped them carry on whenever they began to feel jaded. Throughout her teenage years they had watched her grow. Now, on the eve of her 18th birthday, Rosa was wise beyond her years—wise enough, she considered, to quietly spend more time researching the Spoiler, wanting to present her friends with a fait accompli. And when the nightmares began again and she was screaming the house awake, she was wise enough to know she had to leave the family home. Because they were worse than before; they were half-dreams, half-waking visions. The

Spoiler *was* real. And she was trying to find her way to Rosa.

The train was crowded, as ever. But today was different; one seat remained empty. The woman who sat by the window spent much of the journey watching the landscape slowly changing. But every now and then she'd slowly turn her head to take in her fellow passengers. And when she did, they all felt a shiver go through them, as if all their thoughts were suddenly on show. For once the Spoiler's brightly coloured hair and tattoos were barely noticed — it was that invasive stare that made people uncomfortable. Better to stand or sit in the corridor than next to it.

As for the Spoiler, she was having a wonderful day. Every time she looked around she caught glimpses of people's lives. Surrounded by people, as she was today, it was a pleasing blur, a confusion of faces and events and times. She was not prepared to sort through what she was seeing and deliver tidings, but she was acutely aware that her gaze was causing discomfort. That alone was enough to make the journey worthwhile, but the Spoiler had a specific task to complete, a man to visit. He knew of her and was afraid of her, likewise she had become aware of him a long time ago, when he had been asking questions about her. His attempts to remain unseen by her had been ineffective.

Giovanni Massimo was next on the Spoiler's list.

Rosa had not imagined that she would be living in a friend's front room as she came of age. While most of her schoolmates had gone to University, Rosa's parents were still wringing their hands because they couldn't afford to send her. Rosa had no interest or intention of wasting three years at University. There was far more to be learned outside of such places. Her parents' financial woes and the disruption her night terrors caused made the decision to move out an easy one. The friend, Yolanda, had a job that regularly took her away from home. Rosa knew it was helpful to have someone around the keep an eye on the tiny flat. It made her feel slightly less guilty about having begged the woman to take her in and for the danger she suspected she'd put her in.

So Rosa woke up on her birthday, alone, after a dream where the Spoiler was rooting through Yolanda's books, holding them up one by one and telling Rosa how, in time, they would reduce to dust.

"Everything has a lifespan. Everything needs to die," said the Spoiler. "I could tell you what your lifespan will be. And, more importantly, about how you will get there. Your destination, after all, is the same as everyone else's. The minute details of the journey are where the beauty lies."

Rosa had woken herself up in time to stop the Spoiler detailing the rest of her life. Or had the Spoiler let her go—for now?

Yolanda had left her a birthday cake and Rosa had a slice, ignoring the messages urging her to go drinking later. She needed more than a conventional celebration. The Spoiler's first identifiable words to her, spoken in a dream five years before, came back to her now.

Much more blood to come.

It was a threat, a promise, of a terrifying future. So with the cake, a bottle of wine.

She checked her social media accounts. One post, one question, on each: have you met the Spoiler?

No answers, no comments, no reactions, no 'Likes'. Either no living person on Earth—or at least within the grasp of the Internet—had met the Spoiler, or no one was prepared to talk about it.

It was far too early—barely 6 a.m.—to call Giovanni and Peter, although the wine was telling her to do it anyway. To stop herself, she had one more drink and went for a walk. Even South London was peaceful at this time of day.

Rosa had always feared the transition between night and day. People mistook it for a fear of the night time, but she was not naïve enough to believe that bad things only happened at night. It was the shift between day and night that scared her; the two worlds meeting, overlapping for a time, and then parting until the next dawn or dusk. It was separate from the other parts of the day, a place of unknown possibilities, a daunting prospect rather than an exciting one. Despite her fears, she stepped out into the pre-dawn.

To be drunk—the perfect level of drunk—was something Rosa had only managed to accomplish once or twice. A novice to the art, she was usually too drunk for comfort before she realised she'd had too much. When she'd achieved the perfect level she'd had a wonderful feeling that all kinds of *doors* could be opened. Drinking so early in the day enhanced everything—the focus required to walk in a straight line, the shiver of panic at being slightly out of control—and magnified that lifting of restrictions.

Her phone buzzed; a message from her Facebook account. She nearly didn't read it— another birthday greeting was of no interest her—but when she did, she almost dropped her phone.

I have met the Spoiler.

Rosa quickly checked the sender's profile— Fey Mallaithe was 77 years old, from London, living on the East Sussex coast. It was possible, but unlikely, to be a hoax. Rose did her best to collect her thoughts and messaged the woman back, asking for an interview. The reply came quickly.

It will have to be soon. I will die a week from now.

Rosa was suddenly sober; it seemed some things were even more potent than alcohol.

Rosa had been to Camber Sands as a child, and it seemed strange that people actually lived in a place that looked to have been created solely as a holiday destination. She stood on the endless beach for a while, the wind blowing the train journey from London away. Then she found South Road, and the chalet style bungalow home of Fey Mallaithe.

"I met the Spoiler when I was five years old. She destroyed my life."

The old woman began speaking as soon as she opened the door. Rosa tried not to interrupt;

Fey clearly had no time to waste.

"She didn't tell me I'd meet you," Fey said as she made tea. "But I suppose she couldn't give me every little detail of my life."

"I suppose not," said Rosa, not knowing what else to say. Meeting someone who knew, actually knew, when, where and how they were going to die had rendered her almost speechless. Luckily, Fey was not, and needed only the vaguest of encouragement to tell her story.

"It was during the war, of course," she said. "I lived in London, born and bred just off the Portobello Road. So much damage done there, you'd never know what your street would look like from one day to the next. I was sitting on the front step and a woman came up to me. She looked ordinary enough, although it seemed to me that she wasn't quite *there* in some way. As if she was wearing a costume rather than her normal clothes. I remember her fringe went down to her eyes but I could see she had a red line across her forehead... a tattoo it was, ever so unusual."

She was sitting in a well-worn chair by the window, the sun shining across the lower half of her body, but Rosa knew the old woman was no longer in the room. She was back in West London, reliving that meeting.

"I knew she was the Spoiler, even though I'd never heard the name before. She told me to go with her and I did. In those days you did what adults told you, didn't you?

"She took me to one of the bombed out houses nearby. She sat me down and told me what would happen all through my life. And then she made sure I knew exactly when I would die. It's next Wednesday, at 11.32 in the morning. It's quite peaceful. I suppose I'm lucky. I'll be alone, though. That's the only thing."

Fey's voice faltered for the first time.

"If you knew everything that was going to happen to you, didn't it give you any comfort? Didn't it make you feel secure?" asked Rosa.

Fey was back with her now, glaring. "She took all the mystery out of my life. All the adventure, the *not-knowing*. I knew what jobs I would have, who I would marry, how and when my parents would die. That I would outlive my younger brother."

"Couldn't you change things?" Rosa urged. "Not go for one of the jobs the Spoiler told you you'd get? There must have been a dozen other paths you could have taken, just to prove her wrong. And actually, changing just one thing might have changed everything."

Fey sighed. "Of course I tried. Sometimes I'd forget things she told me until I was doing them. I tried to leave a job before I was supposed to, but somehow I just couldn't. I tried to change what was happening so many times. I tried to forget that I'd met her. It was impossible. In the end I gave up."

Rosa sat back in her chair and gazed towards the sea. It was rough out there, vital. She did not want to look away. There was still a way to thwart fate, to prove the Spoiler was fallible.

"I'll be here with you next Wednesday. When you... go. You won't be alone and it'll show the Spoiler that she doesn't know it all."

"Oh, my dear!" said Fey, her voice cracking with emotion. "Would you really do that for me? Won't the Spoiler be angry?"

"But what could she do to punish you?" asked Rosa. "It's not as if I'm going to stop you from dying."

"I would've thought doing her job would punish *her*," said Fey. "It would make me sad to do what she does."

There was a time when the Spoiler did not enjoy her task. Her appointment had been a trade, a promise of everlasting life if she acted as a messenger for Saimign, a minor demon. It was he who had learned that the human fear of death was a veritable ocean of distress to bathe in, a thing he had cherished for a thousand years. But he had never delivered the messages himself; he appointed an emissary. And in the first half of the 18th century, to his great surprise, a new one had needed to be found. There were plenty of candidates, plenty of miserable wretches who would jump at the chance of wealthy immortality and escape from their hand to mouth existence. To travel the world delivering messages was little to ask in return. But, as the Spoiler found, what she did ruined lives, while her own was unimaginable to the people she met. She travelled on the finest horses wearing the finest clothes, owned a beautiful house and had endless riches; however much she spent, there were always a reassuring amount of gold coins in her purse, although bizarrely never the same amount twice, however carefully she counted them. But it made for a life of luxurious physical comfort. She saw the whole of England and then further, every country in the world, more people and landscapes than anyone in her tiny village could imagine existed, but she brought sadness to everyone she met. It soon filled her with melancholy. She could not bear to do this for the rest of Time. She returned to Saimign and asked to have her previous life restored to her. *At least in that there was only my own misery to live with,* she told him.

Saimign laughed, always a disconcerting thing, his great antlered head thrown back, his hands on his hips. "You're looking at this in the wrong way. Life's short and harsh for your fellows; to be gracious enough to inform them of the details of their lives and the details and manner of their deaths should give them comfort. After all, if they know they're not going to die for many years, that the sickness that sweeps through their village next week will not take them, they're free! It's a human failing to see this knowledge as enslavement. You're a harbinger, a blabbermouth, and it should be celebrated, but if it isn't then it is the burden you must bear."

"But why do this at all? What do you achieve? Is there some personal gain from the misery you cause?"

"I cause nothing!" exclaimed Saimign. "But I learned that misery is a physical thing. At first a trickle of it came my way. I could touch it, taste it. As more humans learned their fate, a tide of misery almost washed me away! It was my gift, to be able to feel these things. You must be open to them. It will enrich your long, long life."

Over time, then, the Spoiler — and Saimign had re-named her, as he had re-named all his emissaries, in order to help her become more than what she had been — became hardened to what she did. She began to see it differently. She began to *enjoy*.

Death became her culture. Her obsession. She knew she was safe from it but at the same time she longed for it and the nothingness she hoped it would bring. Such was her obsession that, at the birth of the 20th Century, which she estimated was her 286th birthday, she had post-mortem cuts tattooed onto her head and body. Many people took them to be tribal designs but now and again someone recognised what they were and reacted with shock. By then she was able to drink in some of those feelings. Not to Saimign's extent, but enough to appreciate his point of view.

Before she became the Spoiler she could have predicted her remaining years without Saimign's help. It would have been the same as any other inhabitant of her village; brutal and yet banal. Life now was something entirely different, a new world with new horizons. Travelling around the globe over the endless years, she was moved to tears at the things she experienced — the Aurora Borealis, an avalanche in the Himalayas, the gnarled, twisted tree-souls of a forest in India, where she walked after delivering messages of hopelessness to both a husband and wife on a nearby farm. It was the first time she'd had the pleasure of destroying two lives at once and some time in the company of the desolate trees was essential for her to enjoy it fully.

She did not consider herself cruel. On the contrary, in the beginning she had dallied with self-pity; she was misunderstood, wilfully so, alone and burdened with her task, but the feeling passed. Most of her instructions from Saimign came via the legion of parasites he had at his command; lice and fleas and tapeworms that would pass on details before burrowing into the nearest dead thing to gorge on it, a sight she never failed to find nauseating. When she told them as such, most were fearfully silent or too busy feasting to care, but one had the gall to turn to her and retort, "Why so appalled? Isn't this exactly what you do?"

She crushed it beneath her boot, of course.

By the time the Spoiler had reached 1940s London and the meeting with Fey Mallaithe, Saimign had long since given her the freedom to give tidings to whomever she pleased, as long as she prioritised his instructions. It was his gift to her, so that she could enjoy her task to the full. One former emissary had begged for the chance of immortality then wasted the time wringing his hands at what he was being asked to do. Things would be different for the Spoiler. Saimign was determined she would be his last appointee.

The Spoiler had spotted Fey playing in the street. Fey was not on her list, but thanks to Saimign, she was able to see the child's life coiling around her like a boa constrictor. The child, of course, was unaware, her arms catching strands of her life as she played. The Spoiler wished she was able to transform herself before approaching the girl, to appear as one of the monsters the girl dreamt about, but she knew that, in this place at this time, anonymity was her best suit. Despite this, there was a moment when Fey glimpsed something alarming about the drab looking woman; her eyes widened momentarily, then relaxed, convinced it was what her mother would call *just your imagination.*

The Spoiler was by now a skilled storyteller; what had begun as dispensing dry facts had become a joy of elaboration. Never lies or exaggeration—there was a way of telling someone their life's story, of dwelling on certain chapters, that made lying unnecessary. Sometimes even the mundane parts had a dramatic effect. Over the years few had doubted that what the Spoiler was telling them was the absolute truth. And now, crushing the dreams of one so young was worth more than the gold coins that never stopped appearing from the purse Saimign had given her.

She often wondered about the rest of her own life. Saimign knew what it would bring, of course, though he would not allow her to see it. She wasn't sure if she believed she would live forever—or at least until the Earth was effectively destroyed, either by a natural or man-made catastrophe. Even after all these years, the concept was beyond her. The glory, or otherwise, of eternal life remained a mystery. Apart from this shadow, however, life was immensely good. The Spoiler felt like the most powerful Being on Earth and beyond; whatever Saimign gained from the despair he spread was diluted, too distant from its source to enjoy fully. Served by his parasite legions, the demon was, frankly, lazy. When the Earth was finally destroyed, he would likely be caught napping and engulfed in flame. The Spoiler imagined being one step ahead, flying into the cosmos to bring tidings to others, for ever, in the endless, wondrous Universe.

What would happen if one of the Spoiler's tidings did not come to pass? Rosa had brought the question up several times over the years with Giovanni and Peter and she thought about it again now, nearly a week after her meeting with Fey. It was possible—easy, almost—to ensure that Fey did not die alone. How this would affect the Spoiler was something they had all only speculated upon, believing up until now that it could never happen.

Now it was about to.

Rosa felt slightly guilty and slightly embarrassed, having caused a spat between the two men. Both were in favour of thwarting the Spoiler—in theory. They had both panicked when Rosa had told them of her meeting with Fey. Excitement, fear and perhaps a little envy had gripped the pair, but her Skyped announcement that she would return to Camber Sands to be with Fey in her last moments had Peter punching the air in delight. Giovanni, however, had looked at him, horrified.

"She can't! The Spoiler will know! We have no idea what will happen. You can't!" he almost shouted.

"She must," said Peter. "We don't know the Spoiler will find out—she could be on the other side of the world right now. What if it weakens her? This is too good an opportunity to miss."

Giovanni gritted his teeth and shook his head.

"Rosa, think carefully about this."

"I already have. I promised I'd go."

To her relief the discussion had been cut short by the sound of their doorbell ringing. Now she was back on the South Coast. At least at Fey's bungalow she had a bed to sleep in, although it was unlikely she'd sleep tonight. She'd never even known someone who'd died, let alone seen a dead body. The thought of being with Fey when she died, perhaps holding her hand, made her feel sick with nerves. But she was taking on the Spoiler. Beating the Spoiler at her own game. And that might give all of them—even Giovanni—some peace of mind.

She took the long route from the bus stop to Fey's home, savouring the sea air.

She had begun dreaming of the Spoiler again.

There was a moment when she almost turned back, when the safer option of leaving well alone looked incredibly attractive, but Fey's obvious relief at seeing her made Rosa glad she'd kept her nerve. Rosa had expected Fey to be panicking, terrified at what was coming—as surely all the Spoiler's victims were—but the woman seemed almost happy.

"I've had a long time to get used to this, my dear. And now that you're going to be here, it will be that much easier."

It seemed Fey had forgiven the Spoiler for what she'd done all those years ago. For her it was not about revenge; she would not be smiling as life slipped away, happy to have got one over on the extraordinary and cruel woman who, somehow, had known everything. Simpler emotions were required; Fey Mallaithe would be content enough to die peacefully, with someone at her side.

Rosa could sense this and was not going to mention the Spoiler but Fey asked what she knew. Rosa got her tablet and showed Fey the Forgotten Folklore website, talked about her long but distant friendship with Peter and Giovanni, like two uncles to her now, and their lifelong fascination with finding the truth behind old legends.

"Do you know what the Spoiler's real name is, my dear?" asked Fey. "She must have had a proper name at one time."

Rosa was caught off guard—Fey saw the Spoiler as innately human, someone who perhaps had been led astray. It was a generous thing to believe. Peter was convinced the Spoiler was many women, generations of the same family, cursed, compelled to spread their terrible news then passing the baton to the next bringer of bad tidings. Rosa had wildly imagined her as a supernatural figure from the distant future, telling people of events that had already occurred. Fey was concerned that she was—almost—an ordinary person caught up in this, even a victim. If the Spoiler had shown remorse for what she did, there was the possibility of having sympathy with her plight. As it was, the woman Rosa knew from her dreams had an aura of delight. Guilt was nowhere to be found.

"If she was someone, a real person, at one

time, it's long gone," she said, and immediately regretted it.

After all, didn't the old woman deserve comfort in her last hours?

"Much more blood to come!" the voice whispered in her ear and Rosa was in the half-sleeping, half-waking state that meant the Spoiler was back again.

"What does that mean?" she spat.

"I told Giovanni the story of his life," was the Spoiler's response.

Everything was in the wrong place. Rosa looked around, disorientated, before remembering where she was. The Spoiler was curled up on top of the bedside cabinet. She sat up, facing the mirror so they could only see each other's faces in reflection. Despite the cold she was still wearing a vest top. She was clearly happy to show off her tattoos and body shape. Rosa grudgingly had to give her credit for that.

The Spoiler followed her gaze and made to take the top off.

"If you want?" she said.

Rosa was embarrassed and angry. "I don't believe you've seen Giovanni. You're lying."

The Spoiler shrugged. "A thousand blood sucking leeches came to me on Lindisfarne and gave me Giovanni Massimo's life story. Giovanni is going insane as we speak. His husband is not far behind."

Rosa glanced at her watch. It was just after 5 o'clock. She grabbed her phone, shaking her head in an attempt to wake up and comprehend what the Spoiler was telling her, but her fugue state continued. She rang Giovanni's number, wondering whether she was really doing it or whether she was dreaming.

Peter answered, and she knew this was more than a dream.

"Has the Spoiler been to your house?"

"It was her at the door when you Skyped us." His voice was slow and colourless.

"Is Giovanni there? Is he alright?"

In answer she heard hearty laughter in the background.

The Spoiler was still there.

She turned and her dream-version of the Spoiler had the biggest smile on her face before she, too, began to laugh.

Rosa couldn't remember if she'd cried when she crept out of the bungalow. She made a thousand excuses in her head but said nothing, the scribbled note she'd left a futile attempt to jolly Fey along to what would be a lonely death after all. It was only when she was waiting at Paddington station for a train heading west that she realised that not only had she let Fey down in the worst way, but the Spoiler's version of the end of Fey's life would come to pass after all.

Fey, however, had cried when she read Rosa's note, but then she pulled herself together, washed and dressed and read the last few pages of a book, sitting in her chair by the window, grateful to feel the sun's warmth on her one last time.

At 11.05 she was overcome with paralysis. It was painless but frightening. The end was not peaceful in the way she had hoped; as she moved from life to death she was met by the piercing screams of a hundred death whistles. Her last thought was that she must be heading to Hell.

In a life of endless travelling, it was a luxury to stop for a while. The Spoiler was enjoying Peter and Giovanni's home; it was something she had not had for more than a century, having dispensed with material symbols of wealth. Her housemates were more like sculptures than people. They barely moved, or spoke, or ate. The few words Peter had spoken to Rosa was the most animated either of them had been since the Spoiler's devastating arrival on their doorstep. The response to her tidings was usually raging anger or grief. This passivity was interesting. And it gave her the chance to sleep, to bathe herself and clean all her clothes, a small rucksack's worth. The house, on the edge of Weston-super-Mare, was more than comfortable. Her involuntary hosts might be in shock for some time yet. Even if they recovered— and they should, given that Giovanni still had more than a quarter of a century left to live—they knew enough to be utterly terrified of her. If they had any sense.

She had been aware of the Forgotten Folklore website for some time. It featured some of the most obscure stories about her and she enjoyed reading it and reminiscing about the past. Was it coincidence that Saimign had chosen one of her biographers? The Spoiler didn't believe in coincidence. It was more likely that Saimign had relished the prospect of the Spoiler coming face to face with the men who presumed to know her.

She dried her face and head, admiring

the line tattooed around her now shaven scalp. There was a tiredness to her face that she didn't like. Despite her surroundings, the Spoiler was not fully rested.

She had been dreaming of Rosa again. The dreams had picked up where they'd left off all those years ago. Rosa was older now, a young woman, and as unhappy to see the Spoiler as the Spoiler was to see her. It was inconvenient and inexplicable, although her dream-self never let it show. She was wilder in that state, a snarling animal capable of climbing walls and running, upside down, across ceilings. But it had been fun to tell Rosa that she'd given tidings to a friend. The Spoiler was only vaguely aware that Rosa had been with Fey Mallaithe at the time of the latest dream, so assured was she that Fey's death would be exactly as she'd reported it all those years ago. Rosa's whereabouts, then, were nothing to worry about, but the dreams were making life more difficult and needed to be dealt with.

Peter and Giovanni's cat had taken a liking to her, as most cats did, and the Spoiler climbed onto the kitchen counter to sit next to it. She must have fallen asleep; the next thing she was aware of was the doorbell ringing. Giovanni stood up slowly and shuffled out to answer it.

The Spoiler smiled. She knew who it would be.

Once every decade Saimign would order some of his parasites to fetch the Spoiler to him. He felt it reasserted his authority over her. There was also the joy of hearing, first hand, exactly how people had reacted to his tidings. On this occasion, the summer of 1974, the Spoiler had been travelling through Mexico. She'd pulled her beautiful but lumbering Ford over to relieve herself in the dusty nothingness and found herself surrounded by grotesque hookworms urging her to go with them. She shook off the ones who were making their way up her leg. One had made it further up and she saw its smooth body arching, mouth open in an attempt to clamp onto her skin, as it fell off her forehead.

The demon had made his home in an underground cavern that was as beautiful as it was repulsive. Gigantic white crystals criss-crossed the ceiling and stood at every angle, some leaning as if in the process of falling. Their whiteness picked out and magnified the tiny chinks of light in the cavern, making the hideous cave spiders visible, each one twelve inches across but capable of slipping in and out of the smallest cracks. Saimign loved it all, sitting majestically in a boiling pool of misery. It bubbled and spat, and stank of effluence. The Spoiler was confident enough in the demon's company to look at the pool in disdain. Each thought the other a fool.

"My previous emissaries were far more respectful," said Saimign. "One could say fearful, of me."

He grinned, knowing how dreadful he looked to her. In all these years he had never mentioned anyone else carrying out his duties. This was a shocking revelation. She tried to remain expressionless.

"Did you really think you were unique? Two have been before you. Weak men, both of them. One fell in love and managed to kill himself when his beloved died. That's when I chose you. The other is still alive and working for me, although he's not aware of it."

The Spoiler was furious. How did she not know this?

"He changed," Saimign continued. "His body and mind were affected by his duties. He stays in one place now, making gravestones for the villagers—while they're still alive. It's his way of giving them tidings. As you can imagine, the Stonemason's work is rarely appreciated."

The Spoiler had meant to find the Stonemason; partly out of curiosity, partly from resentment, but the years passed and she never seemed to find time. Besides, Saimign himself said he was a weak soul, unable to leave his village or even tell people any more than the date of their death.

But now, more than four decades later, in the home of her petrified hosts, she had found a reference to him; just a line on the Forgotten Folklore website, which she traced to a pamphlet in their library. A cheaply produced set of photocopied sheets, it described the folklore of Northumberland and made a reference to the Stonemason, who had terrorised a village by making gravestones for the living. No one had made the link between him and her. The Spoiler wondered again if she should visit him. But for now the Massimos' library provided a fascinating, sometimes amusing, read. It almost made up for the restless, dreaming nights.

Peter and Giovanni's perception of Time had been altered by the arrival of the Spoiler. They were both aware that days had passed, but that ordinary Time belonged to the world outside their home. The shock of seeing the Spoiler face to face, of having the rest of Giovanni's life laid out before them had become an endless, hideous moment. Peter, especially, was aware that he needed to wake from his altered state, not only to support Giovanni, but to live in and change the present and future if he could, but the Spoiler's continued presence, the ownership she'd taken of their home, was making it impossible. Fear and sadness was choking them both.

The Spoiler, too, was aware that the two men were caught in slow motion. She was used to being in a different frame of Time to everyone, and everything, else, with all life speeding along, hurtling past her towards death. Her hosts, she knew, would return to normal Time but for now it was interesting to watch them.

For Rosa Rugosa, Giovanni opening his door to her was like the curtain going up on the performance of a nightmare. They had not met before. It should have been joyous; old friends meeting for the first time. Instead, it was a wake for a man who had not yet died.

They hugged her; slowly, as if movement was new to them. But there was love in the embrace.

"You shouldn't have come," whispered Peter, eyes wide in fright. "She's here. And you shouldn't have to see us like this."

Behind them the Spoiler rose, still on the kitchen counter.

"Oh, I don't know, boys," she said, enjoying the sound of her own voice. "Weston has a great energy about it; many Occultists have made this their home. It's not the banal town in pretends to be." She towered over them. "Besides, it's me she's really come to see."

Rosa studied the Spoiler. The woman had dogged her all her life, in dreams and in her half-sleeping state. This was the first time that Rosa knew she was fully awake, fully in control of what she said and did. The Spoiler, now bald and brazenly displaying her autopsy tattoos, was clearly expecting—and relishing—this meeting. And both knew that Rosa was no match for her.

Rosa did her best to comfort Giovanni, although for a young woman who had barely seen life and couldn't comprehend death, it was near to impossible. She struggled to find the right words—as if there could be right words, a magical combination that would make everything better.

"We've been naïve," said Peter. "All this time, learning about these legends, these strange people, we never imagined any of this would be used against us. Does that mean we never really believed in any of it? Or did we put ourselves above it all?"

Tired of Peter's self-indulgence, the Spoiler jumped down from the counter.

"You all know me, a little, anyway," she said. "And yet you don't know me at all. I've spoken to Rosa many times—but you never understood the language, did you?"

Rosa hated her more than ever. The Spoiler picked a knife from the block and offered it to her.

"For what harm it will do me."

Despite their inertia, Peter and Giovanni

reacted to the revelation that Rosa had met the Spoiler.

"I've dreamt of her since I was a child," she explained. "That's why I first got in touch with you. I wanted to find out if she was real."

Peter turned to the Spoiler. "You said she didn't understand the language you spoke. What language was it?" he asked in his slurred, slowed down voice.

In reply, the Spoiler opened her mouth and began a strange whistling and trilling, so similar to a bird's call that the cat opened its eyes and sat up.

"It is one of the oldest languages on Earth. And almost extinct," said the Spoiler. "It's only spoken in dreams now."

Realising Rosa was not going to take the knife, the Spoiler crossed the room at speed and held the blade at Peter's throat.

"Ask me a question, Rosa!" she said.

Rosa's mind went blank. Then was full with a thousand questions; all contained in one.

"Who *are* you?"

The Spoiler shrugged. She let Peter go and sat down.

"You mean—who was I? Around four hundred years ago I was Breone Widdowson, a peasant, barely surviving in a village in Herefordshire. When I was a child I was told stories of a dragon that would come and drink from the river nearby. I believe that story now, but for a long time I stopped believing in things like that, after my brother and sister died from disease. Short, cruel lives are wonderful ways to stop people believing in magic. Good magic, that is; everyone in my village believed in curses, in demons. I thought I was going to Hell when I met one. But instead, he saved me."

Giovanni sighed. And Rosa was angry, again, at the Spoiler.

"And the cost of that has been paid by God knows how many people over the years," she said.

The Spoiler leant forward, her eyes glinting. "If people accepted their own mortality, their fate, then I'd have no power over them." She pointed at Giovanni. "Your friend here is a perfect example. He's been given the meaning of his life, yet he sits there and drowns. Cowards, all of you. Saimign bathes in your fear and misery."

Rosa steeled herself. The Spoiler had revealed a lot, but not what Rosa desperately needed to know. She was unprepared for what she would hear but needed to hear it anyway. Wasn't that the reason the Spoiler had stayed on in Weston? Wasn't that what she was leading up to?

"We both know that you know the rest of my life," she began. "'Much more blood to come', you said to me a long time ago. I've thought of nothing else for years. Tell me the rest. I'm not afraid."

The lie was not convincing.

The Spoiler lit up. Of course! She'd told Rosa part of her story. She only knew part of it, but there was no need for Rosa to know that. For the first time, she faced someone who was prepared to know everything. Everyone else had done their best to run away from it. Rosa was indeed extraordinary

The Spoiler watched her, feeling her dread and impatience, savouring them.

And then—inspiration.

The Spoiler shook her head, the light bouncing off it, her appearance more alien than human.

"Some things you just have to wait for. Your life will unfold before you as you go. You know part of it. But where? When? How? There is a beauty in not knowing. You will see that. Eventually."

Rosa grabbed the Spoiler by the shoulders.

"No! I've lived with this for far too long. You must tell me now. That is your job. Your purpose."

They were close now, face to face. The Spoiler allowed Rosa's hands to remain on her. It was agreeably intimate.

"My task is to deliver Saimign's tidings. And I have done—to Giovanni Massimo. You are not on my list. You may never be. So you'll know nothing until it happens."

She gently removed herself from Rosa's grasp, went to the garden and lit a cigarette, a rare treat, in celebration. She was elated. After all her years on Earth, the Spoiler had learned something new, something she was sure Saimign did not know; that not revealing something could be as joyous as revealing everything. She would meet Rosa again and again—this was obvious to them both—but it was necessary now to move on, to leave Rosa with the only thing worse than knowing her fate. She would be almost sad to leave; being here was, she imagined, like being part of a family.

She watched the crescent moon rise. It was late in the night when she went indoors to pack.

Pig Iron

When Elizabeth Longbarrow was 38 years old, she began to turn invisible.

It happened slowly, creeping like the change of the seasons. One day she noticed that her reflection in the bathroom mirror had faded. The mirror was dirty, so she cleaned it. Her reflection didn't change but the mirror was old, so she assumed there was something wrong with it—perhaps the backing was peeling away—but then she found that she looked the same in all the mirrors in the house. She cleaned them all, but it made no difference; her eyebrows looked lighter than usual, her eyes misty.

Soon she faded a little more. She wondered if it was her imagination. Her clothes looked washed-out when she wore them, fresh and new when she took them off. It wasn't the sort of thing she could go to a doctor about and it was too bizarre to talk to anyone about, so she kept it to herself.

As time went on, she realised other people had noticed. Her husband began to refer to her as Eliza, then Liz, as if her failing solidity should be reflected in her name. Still she didn't talk about it. How could she bring up such a subject? She was able to see through parts of her body—

not clearly, as if through glass, but blurred light and objects could definitely be seen through her hands and thighs. At the next family gathering she was barely acknowledged and no one asked after her. When she spoke, it was in a voice so faint that she hardly heard her own words. Before long, her calls and emails to friends were going unanswered. Daniel, such an attentive husband, began to act as if she wasn't there, avoiding conversation with her most of the time. And one day he stopped referring to her at all.

That was the day she decided to leave.

"I have become a ghost in my own life," she cried in her tiny voice. No one would notice that she was no longer there. Grief-stricken, she wrote a note for Daniel, but the text faded before her eyes. What did it matter? He had not tried to save her. She left the house through the back door, meaning to savour the garden she'd always loved then be out the back gate and away, along the alleys that ran behind the houses.

She had no idea of where she was going. As long as she was away from here, from Enfield, she really didn't care.

The old woman settled down on the bench and gazed across the field. The bench, dedicated to a man who had similarly loved the view, was comfortable and she thanked him for his thoughtfulness in providing a place for her to sit, as she always did when she was there. She had seen foxes, buzzards and more rabbits than she could count from the bench over the years. Her eyesight was not so good these days, but on a fine day such as this she could see perfectly well.

Which was why she blinked and rubbed her eyes when the view on her left hand side bent and distorted. The field, and the crows pecking in the grass, were still there, but their proportions had changed. The left hand side cleared and the distortion moved across to the right.

Something was moving in front of her. Mary Uffington picked up her stick and waved it around. It hit an object.

"I see you!" she shouted. It was a half-truth. The distortion moved until it was on the bench next to her. She could just make out a human shape, then a miniature human voice.

"I didn't think anyone could see me any more," it said. A female voice; frightened and sad by the sound of it.

"Perhaps they're not trying hard enough," said Uffington.

"I don't understand what's happened to me," said Elizabeth, grateful for someone to talk to but closer to panic now that she could express herself.

"We all fade from sight now and then," said Uffington kindly. "But your situation seems to be permanent. Have you been cursed, I wonder?"

Elizabeth didn't think so. Who would bother to curse her?

Uffington thought for a moment. "I could stitch you a suit of skin," she offered. "It would give you a reflection at least. It wouldn't be your own face, of course, but it might reassure you of your own existence."

Elizabeth's eyes widened at the thought, although the offer had been made with the best of intentions.

"Why aren't you frightened of me?" she asked. "You seem very unconcerned that an invisible woman's sitting next to you."

Uffington turned to her, wishing she could see Elizabeth's features rather than this faint sketch of a person.

"I've been called many things in my life," she said. "Witch. Harlot. Drunkard. Spoiler... But I take these accusations to mean that I'm open minded. And no one's ever called me a coward. You are frightened, but not frightening. Answer me one thing—do you want to remain as you are?"

"Of course not," Elizabeth tried to shout.

"I thought I'd ask. There are probably all kinds of advantages to being invisible. But I know of a person who might be able to help. You need to seek an audience with Jasper, the Ashen Queen. Follow me."

Elizabeth was about to ask why a queen would have a man's name but Uffington was off the bench and heading back along the track towards her home, so she followed, marvelling at the way her feet squashed the grass, how the gate at the edge of the field opened and clicked shut at her invisible touch.

Uffington's home turned out to be a caravan on a quiet patch of land belonging to a benevolent friend whose home was screened by apple trees. It was only a couple of miles from the outskirts of Enfield, itself on the outskirts of London.

"It's hot in summer, cold in winter, but I wouldn't live anywhere else. I have peace here and my friend's cats come to visit when the mood takes them."

They sat in the caravan and drank tea. Uffington was amazed at the way her cup and saucer began to disappear in Elizabeth's hands, then became solid again when they were set on the table.

"Most people," said Uffington, "only see part of what's in front of their faces, what surrounds them all their lives. Hence you being a ghost in your own life... "

Elizabeth nearly dropped her cup at Uffington's choice of words.

"The Ashen Queen lives in the Unfortunate Forest. My *shew-stone* is the only way of finding it."

She took the teacups away and placed what looked like a large pendant in front of Elizabeth. It was black and quite ominous looking. Elizabeth stared at its highly polished surface and was only just aware of Uffington lighting a sweet-smelling incense stick. She didn't know what a shew-stone was but there was something fascinating about it, so she kept staring into it.

After an amount of time that she couldn't gauge—she was admonished whenever her focus drifted away from the stone—she saw flashes of her own face. It was as she remembered it; pale, beginning to acknowledge its age. It changed, flowing seamlessly back in time, until she was young, a teenager. No lines on this flesh, but no wisdom, either. The years raced forward and she was her own age again for a few glorious moments before her features became transparent once more.

Then she saw a forest, its trees bending

over, leaning towards her. An Avenue ran through the trees, constructed from thousands of gigantic pieces of quartz, carved thousands of years ago from the boulders that lay on the forest floor.

Then there was just the draughty caravan again and an empty space in the stone where her reflection should have been.

Uffington was nodding happily. "The shew-stone suits you," she said.

"What does it do?" asked Elizabeth.

"You've just seen what it does. It relays messages and signs from other places. You saw the forest?"

"Yes. It had a kind of road running through it."

"That's wonderful. It means we'll find our way to it. It was by no means a foregone conclusion, you see."

"We? You're coming with me?" Elizabeth, still unsure how much of this she believed, was nonetheless moved at the older woman's kindness.

"If I'm with you in the forest, you've less chance of being killed."

Elizabeth gawped. Uffington had a habit of announcing horrors in the most casual way. She began to ask how far they'd have to travel but Uffington ushered her to the door.

Outside the caravan lay the Unfortunate Forest.

The Middlesex countryside had disappeared. The apple trees that gave Uffington privacy had been replaced by woodland that crept almost to the door. It looked beautiful and romantic and forbidding all at once. Elizabeth turned to Uffington and studied her expression. It was ominously unreadable.

"We'd better get on, then," was all she said, picking up a walking stick that hung from the door handle and setting off into the trees.

"Hi! Are you with me? Don't hang back. Talk to me so I know you're there," she shouted.

Elizabeth caught up with her and apologised.

"I keep wondering if there was something I did to cause this," she said. "I go over everything I did in the days before I noticed I was fading away. There has to be a reason for this happening to me."

Uffington glared at the barely discernable shape beside her. "We women blame ourselves for all the ills of the world," she said. "Malignant influences are all around us. Let's not become one of them."

Elizabeth nodded, hoping Uffington could see her.

"Why is this called the Unfortunate Forest?"

Uffington's reply was ominously vague.

"Everything I've heard about this place is from storytellers. Probably some distance from the truth, I would think."

And as they walked, the trees behind them bent over, as if to obstruct the way out.

The forest was not beautiful. To describe it as such would be to redefine beauty. The Unfortunate Forest was nature at its most savage in a ruthless fight for survival. Different realities merged and clashed, a reaction more violent than all the Earth's volcanos erupting at once. Ancient English oaks fought for space amongst wild Indian fig trees with roots that flowed like lava. Other trees, the like of which no one had ever seen, grew around the trunks of both, attempting to strangle them. Where the sun penetrated a canopy that writhed and thrashed in battle, strange flowers grew.

Nature was not harmonious here. The only part of the forest that remained constant was the Avenue, held in place by a will that was stronger than the chaos that surrounded it. The Avenue, dazzlingly bright wherever the sun caught it, eventually led to the Mountain of Vagaries, a place where nothing could be relied upon. It was the birthplace of Jasper, the Ashen Queen. She had no control over the trees and plants but her subjects, who lived in the forest or roamed the mountain when food was scarce, were loyal.

They were known as the Beasts. And food was now plentiful, for inside the forest, wrapped tight in a grove of misshapen trees and shadowed by vegetation, were the houses of a street in Enfield that were simultaneously bathed in sunshine in the world Elizabeth Longbarrow had left behind.

A boulder the size of a car rolled effortlessly through the trees, stopping only when it crashed into an enormous tree root resting on the ground. As one, Elizabeth and Uffington stepped up onto the Avenue, the only constant in the chaos. Nothing here moved, now or ever, it seemed. Perhaps that was the Avenue's purpose.

"This place was named by an Englishman,"

said Elizabeth. "Who else would've made such an understatement?"

Uffington laughed. She could hear Elizabeth more clearly now. It was just a matter of tuning in.

They walked for a while in silence, both wondering what the forest held and how they'd find the Ashen Queen. The trees became denser, packed together in morbid crowds. They looked damaged here, twisted by disease, but still alive, even thriving. Elizabeth, overwhelmed by new experiences, looked away but Uffington wanted to see into the darkness—if there was danger, she wanted to be forewarned.

Uffington, then, saw why the trees here were twisted. She saw the houses, tree trunks wrapped around them, squeezing them like a snake squeezes its prey. Branches pushed their way through doors and windows, destroying beloved family photographs and prized possessions as they swarmed around the rooms. Elizabeth, alerted by her new friend's cry of alarm, recognised them. The trees had the houses in their grip; brick, glass and wood shuddered and shattered but many of the rooms were almost intact. Inside were the occupants, in various states of injury. Limbs were twisted, crushed or torn off, chests peeled away to view pumping hearts, orifices opened and explored. They remained untouched by the trees, however.

Flesh and blood was in the hands of the Beasts.

The Beasts were allowed free rein with humans. Jasper, the Ashen Queen had no interest in either the buildings or the occupants and besides, she was aware that even the most loyal subjects might rebel if they were hungry enough.

In another time, the Beasts had been human, too. But, like everything else here, they were *altered*. Most of the time they resembled skeletons and it was only close up that skin could be seen, dry and stretched, doing its best to cover the bones. They remained in this state unless they were feeding, when they became so swollen they were unrecognisable; the Beasts were unable to control themselves once they'd begun.

The Beasts were from another time, but not from another place. The houses and their unhappy residents, however, dwelt simultaneously in the Unfortunate Forest and in Middlesex Road, Enfield, although each was unaware of the other's existence. If the residents of Middlesex Road were in pain or felt melancholic, they'd shrug their shoulders and consider it inevitable, the price paid for modern life and material success. That another version of their selves existed at all was beyond their imagination. Similarly, the terrified and tortured residents of the shattered houses would not benefit from knowing of the comfortable lives lived by their *others*.

The Beasts, however, were eternally joyful creatures, at their happiest just before beginning a meal. The anticipation was full of ritual and wildly exciting, at least as good as the meal itself. The Beasts lifted their heads and began to speak, as they liked to do, as one:

"*Here we Beasts do dwell,*
In Exquisite starvation,

The Ashen Queen's servants,
About to feed and replenish.
A swollen belly is good for the Soul."

Their voices screeched, screamed and squealed the words. As with everything they said, it was almost a song, the harmonies clashing and the melody twisted. Some of the Beasts repeated certain words, special to them, in their screaming voices.

Elizabeth turned away from the sound. "These are my neighbours! The whole road's here."

Uffington made a guess as to where Elizabeth's arm would be, and grabbed it. "I'm guessing that your road and your neighbours are where they've always been. Many of us are in two places at once. I suspect that you, however, will have escaped. Bless your luck for being invisible. I knew it would have its advantages," she said.

"But Daniel will be here, won't he?" said Elizabeth. She twisted out of Uffington's grasp and jumped off the Avenue so as to get closer to the houses.

They were in the same order, the same position as they were in Enfield. Elizabeth squeezed around the trees and made her way to her house. It was like walking home in a dream.

The sight of her home in the tree's crushing grip made her lose her balance momentarily. The house looked almost undamaged but stood at an angle. How could her home in Middlesex Road be still there, co-existing with this aberration but untouched and unaware? She climbed along a branch to the smashed lounge window.

Daniel was not inside. The furniture had

slid to one side of the room. Ivy covered the sofa, bindweed was wrapped tightly around the television, insects crawled over the cushions. A sound came from the upper floor of the house; a cry of utter despair.

It was Daniel. She scrabbled further along the branch, desperate to get inside and help him but was hooked back. Uffington was on the ground, waving her stick around.

"You can't go in there. The last thing you want is for those Beasts to notice you."

"Daniel needs my help," Elizabeth wailed.

"He hasn't done much to help *you*, from what I've heard," replied Uffington. "Anyway, I'm sure the man you know is happily going about his business in Enfield. This is too much to take on. We came here to make you visible again. If we can."

As they continued along the Avenue, both women had the same thought: if Elizabeth could be made visible again, what would she do?

Elizabeth spoke first.

"If I can get back to normal, I'm not sure I'd go running back home. I faded from view there, from their lives. And no one seemed too concerned about it. My friends, my family, were looking through me. No one tried to stop it."

"Well, that's something to consider," said Uffington. "But the modern world hasn't got time to understand anything out of the ordinary. We've lost the ability to wonder."

"You haven't."

"Yes, but I became a recluse to avoid becoming an outcast. Perhaps by the time we find the Ashen Queen, you'll want to stay as you are. Now, I wonder where she is. I wouldn't be surprised if she's watching us right now."

Jasper was indeed watching the two women. She was seated on her throne, listening with intense pleasure to the sounds of her kingdom, and in her mind's eye was an image from the Avenue of one elderly female witch and the suggestion of someone else—unless the old woman was talking to herself or the human-shaped distortion in the air was a natural phenomenon. Both were quite possible.

The Ashen Queen's throne was a colossal stone with natural dips that so resembled a seat with head and arm rests that it had, according to folklore, been shaped by skilled hands for some long-lost deity. It had been dragged down from the Mountain of Vagaries and set in the Unfortunate Forest several hundred years ago for former monarchs. Jasper adored the throne. She adored rock. She hoped that when she died she would *become* rock and would sit on the Mountain of Vagaries forever.

Until then there was life to revel in, a forest kingdom to rule and the question of the traveller—or travellers—on the Avenue. Should she grant them safe passage? After all, the Beasts already had plenty to eat. She settled back into her throne. The rock was hot.

The throne was guiding her. She should meet the travellers and decide their fate, although she was minded to spare them; to travel through the forest was an act of bravery, foolishness or desperation. The reputation of the Beasts, of course, put humans, animals, even certain flora off from living or growing in the forest and so visitors were rare.

The termite hill nearest the throne, a grand, soaring mound, had no such reluctance. Its many fingers reached towards the sky, seething with life. Jasper ordered its millions of workers to form the shape of a cushioned travel chair and she reclined, in comfort, as the termites took her to the Avenue.

The sight was astonishing. A hint of movement way back in the trees became a shape carefully manoeuvring around roots, boulders and snatching flower traps. When it turned towards the Avenue and found a ray of sunlight, it revealed a supremely confident looking woman seated on a dark, living chair that transported her towards the two women. Boulders rolled close by but wisely avoided the undulating form.

Neither Uffington or Elizabeth were in any doubt as to who the woman was. Elizabeth studied her carefully.

The Ashen Queen was magnificent. Despite being seated, she was clearly extremely tall; at least seven feet, Elizabeth guessed. She wore a dress that shimmered between green and blue and despite her almost silvery skin looked at the peak of health. Noting her broad, muscular frame, Elizabeth remembered her name and wondered if the Ashen Queen was actually female or a transvestite. Or transgender. She wasn't sure of the difference and was not inclined to ask.

Some of the insects that made up her travel chair were crawling over her dress and through her mass of mauve hair. Somehow it didn't sully her and she did not seem disturbed by it.

Jasper, in turn, looked Uffington over; a witch who was long past her best. No threat there. The Other, however, was interesting. It was camouflaged, all but invisible. Jasper's careful eye caught Elizabeth's shape. She sniffed the air and detected a female smell. It was impressive. The witch might have something about her after all.

"Is the invisibility spell your work, witch?"

Uffington gave a self-conscious curtsey. "I can't take credit for it, I'm afraid, Your Majesty. The source of my friend's state is unknown. She would beg you to return her to her usual state."

Jasper raised her eyebrows. "I could do so, I don't doubt. But should I? Tell me, invisible woman, what is your favourite stone?"

Elizabeth went blank. Then she looked at the Ashen Queen's hair and remembered a stone her mother had set into a ring.

"Amethyst, Your Majesty."

"Hmm. Amethyst can deceive. Another."

Elizabeth was desperate to find the right answer. Then inspiration hit her.

"The shingle beach at Lyme Regis. We went there on holiday so many times. I loved the place. My favourite stone is a pebble—any pebble—off that beach. I've no idea what they're made of."

Jasper smiled. "That's better. An honest answer, and a very good one."

Elizabeth had intended being patient, to grovel if need be in order to reverse her condition, but her distress at what she had seen in the trees was overwhelming.

"My husband and my neighbours—my whole street—are in those trees. It's disgusting. Why the fuck are you letting that happen?"

The Ashen Queen got up and stepped across from the termite chair to the Avenue. If anything she was taller than Elizabeth had first thought. Uffington winced, sure that Elizabeth would be punished for her remark, but she was only staring at the space where Elizabeth stood.

"I do so wish I could see your face, your expression," she said. "What is in those trees is not quite as it appears."

"I did speculate that what was in the trees was another version of her home, which probably hasn't moved an inch from where it's always been," said Uffington.

"Your friend was right," said Jasper, still staring towards Elizabeth. "The people you saw in the trees became detached from the version you know. *Air Leth*—separated souls—are uncommonly common. More than you would care to know. They live their lives in times and worlds different to the one you know. They're of you but apart from you. Such a mass separation, though, is rare. The Beasts usually find people in here alone. No wonder they're ecstatic."

Elizabeth wasn't sure she believed either of them. She imagined Middlesex Road suddenly devoid of houses, front gardens with paths leading to nothing, the residents reported en masse as missing. But if the Ashen Queen—and Uffington—were right, it would be a miracle; the Daniel she knew and still loved wouldn't be the man making those desperate sounds. But she would need to return to Enfield to be convinced.

Meanwhile, there was her own situation to contend with. The Ashen Queen was taking long, deep breaths, her eyes closed, enjoying the presence of everything around her. She held out her hands.

"Take my hands, woman. I know you're there but I want to feel you."

The Ashen Queen hadn't taken offence at her outburst. With great relief Elizabeth reached up and let her hands be enclosed. It sent a shudder through her. It was the touch of termites, of stone, tree bark, earth and grasses. The trees huddled around them, lowering their branches in honour. The Beasts encircled them, mewing and fawning in their sing-song voices.

Then they were back on the Avenue and all was as it had been. Except that it wasn't. Everything had changed. The colours of the Ashen Queen's dress shimmered more brilliantly, the sun shone through the forest canopy more brightly. Uffington raised her eyebrows and Jasper gave a knowing smile.

"Come back to the grove with me," she said, stepping back across to her travel chair. "I'll show you the people you think are your neighbours. And your husband! You'll see how similar, but how different they are. And then we'll discuss how you'll repay me when I make you visible again."

The Ashen Queen was confident. It gave Elizabeth hope; now was not forever. The life she'd lived in Enfield seemed like a utopia compared to this. Whatever the Ashen Queen asked for in return would be worth giving. She was beckoning for them to stand on the back of the travel chair. The thought of standing on millions of insects was abhorrent but Elizabeth couldn't risk offending her host. She closed her eyes and stepped onto the swarming mass, feeling each termite as it moved under her feet, then helped Uffington step across. Uffington was clearly fazed, but was doing her best not to look it.

The chair circled and made its way back towards the grove. From her position, high up on the back of the chair, Elizabeth began to see the Unfortunate Forest in a different light. There was woodland near her home and she and Daniel had often walked through it, but she'd never thought of it as a living entity. Here it was impossible to see it in any other way; even the air was charged with life. Now she was on the chair Uffington seemed to be enjoying the experience a little more. She had her stick hooked over her shoulder, not wanting to stab the termites, and held on to the back of the chair for balance, the handkerchief around her hand failing to cushion the sensation of the insects underneath.

A boulder rolled close to the chair and the termites slowed a little and manoeuvred to avoid it.

"I'd prefer to walk, really," said the Ashen Queen, "but everything here has such an old fashioned idea of how to treat a queen."

They were close to the grove. Both Elizabeth and Uffington were dreading seeing the tortured souls inside the houses again, but there was no choice. To make things worse, one of the Beasts, a spider making its way across the landscape of its ribs, was waiting for them. It reached up and helped the Ashen Queen down to the forest floor.

"Show us some of the people here," she told it.

A sing-song chorus came from the grove and all the houses in Middlesex Road in reply.

"Wondrous Majesty,
All that we have is yours.
You may end our miserable lives, tear our bones from our bodies,
Or you may let us live as you see fit."

The sound made the two outsiders wince. As it faded away the wails of the Beasts' prisoners took over. Elizabeth's bowels churned and Uffington clasped her stick more tightly, but their urge to know the truth kept them a few paces behind the Ashen Queen and her simpering subject.

They stopped at the nearest house. The Andersons had lived there for a decade, their children having fledged a few years back. Elizabeth hoped they had been spared. John Anderson was visible through the kitchen window. A Beast had one skinny hand around the back of his neck, the other gripped his stomach, squeezing his intestines. Needle-like appendages reached from its shoulders. Most were inserted into Anderson's body; into one eye, through his chest, into his temple. One of the free appendages moved as they watched, piercing one cheek and, moments later, appearing out of the other. The man looked over at them, his agony increasing at the sight of the Ashen Queen. There was no hint of recognition on his face and it took Elizabeth a few moments to remember that he couldn't see her. She wondered if he would know her if she was visible—would the Air Leth version of John Anderson have the same memories?

They left the man to his fate and continued along the hellish version of Middlesex Road. At last they reached Elizabeth's house. To Elizabeth's disgust the Beast led the way through her home. It was clearly familiar with the building. It stopped halfway up the stairs, the wall having been breached by a heavy tree branch. The hole resembled a wound, with bricks hanging precariously, ready to fall. The Beast stretched its scrawny body across the danger area and beckoned the Ashen Queen up the stairs. It returned to the Ashen Queen's side as soon as she was past. Uffington snorted at this rudeness, but the women continued to the top of the stairs without incident.

Daniel was being held in the bedroom. He was lying on the bed, covered by a sheet. The room was exact in every detail—the photos on the dressing table, the paintings on the wall. If this was a copy, it was a convincing one. She didn't want to look at Daniel but knew she would have to.

The Beast had left the Ashen Queen's side and was at the bed, snatching away the sheet with obvious enthusiasm. Daniel was being embraced by one of the Beasts. The Beast—the same height as Daniel but so skinny its shape had not stood out under the sheet—was so close to him that they seemed physically attached. Daniel's clothes— always classic, expensive—were shredded and covered in blood and other muck. Daniel's head, the only part of him not clasped by the Beast, turned and gazed at the visitors. And Elizabeth was sure that this was not her Daniel. It was a fake, a carbon copy. Perhaps it was his eyes that gave it away; there was no depth to them. She wanted to cry for this man but her relief that this was not her husband made her almost sick.

The house, the street, the people inside who she'd known for years—they all existed in two places. Except, possibly, for her. Although –

"*Is* there an invisible version of me here?"

"There might be," said the Ashen Queen. "Becoming invisible might mean you're here but you've escaped the Beasts. But then it's also possible that you've never been here. You may be somewhere else, or perhaps not even have an Air Leth soul."

Uffington cleared her throat. "Well, there's no need for us to stay here any longer," she said. "Can we go elsewhere, Your Majesty, to discuss whether my friend can be made visible again?"

Jasper turned her gaze from the bed.

"Indeed," she said. "We'll go to the palace. There's much to discuss."

And what will this palace be made of? thought Uffington as they made their way out of the house. *Mud? Mosquitos?* She could not imagine it would be the kind of palace royalty usually lived in. Uffington was out of her depth. A lifetime of strange experiences hadn't prepared her for the Unfortunate Forest. She had heard of it and of Jasper, the Ashen Queen, only in stories and rumours and had never had reason to attempt to find either until now. The relative ease with which Elizabeth had seen it in the shew-stone had been as unnerving as it was exciting. Uffington wasn't sure what she thought of the Ashen Queen. For the present she was co-operating, which Uffington was grateful for. Her influence over Elizabeth, however, was a little worrying. What would she ask for in return for making Elizabeth visible again?

They zig-zagged through the forest on the termite chair, avoiding boulders and the more unwieldy roots. When they reached the throne, Jasper dismounted. As the others followed suit, she ordered the termites to disperse. The chair melted onto the forest floor. The termites streamed back to their towering mound. Uffington marvelled at the throne; its beautiful back and arm rests were too ornate to have been carved by anything other than the wind, the rain and time itself.

Jasper's palace stood behind the giant stone. When Elizabeth saw it she couldn't help but feel a twinge of disappointment. Someone of the Ashen Queen's stature—in all senses of the word—was worth more than the building that stood in the small clearing. It was circular, and looked like a child's messy outdoor den, although it was decorated with big, colourful spirals, which was quite pleasing. Uffington, however, was struck with amazement. The palace had been constructed from the living roots of the nearby trees. They had been trained and shaped—either by nature or by hand, human or otherwise—to make an elaborate building. And the painted walls were beautiful. It was perfect. Other, smaller structures stood nearby. Uffington guessed they had ritual use.

Jasper began towards the round house.

"When you return home," she said, looking carefully at the space made by Elizabeth as she walked, "will you treat your husband differently now you've seen another version of him? Will you pity your neighbours, knowing that a part of them will be suffering and dying?"

"I don't know how I'll feel," said Elizabeth. "But I can't see how they don't know what's going on back there."

"Just assume that they're oblivious and be thankful of it," said Uffington. "I knew of the Air Leth but I've never seen them with my own eyes before. I've never pursued how many other Mary Uffingtons there might be and I certainly won't be doing so in the future. Sometimes wisdom lies in not knowing something."

Jasper stopped at the door of the palace.

"You," she said to Uffington, "can go home now. Your friend is safe with me. She'll be returned when I'm finished with her."

She was being dismissed. Uffington was suspecting the Ashen Queen's motives, as well as her morals. She was torn. This experience was the most revelatory of her lifelong dabbling in magic and she dearly wanted to stay, but it would be unwise to refuse such an order.

What happened next forced her hand. A gust of wind tore through the canopy above. A loud crack alerted her to a heavy branch hurtling down towards her.

"Away with you!" she shrieked and thrust her stick at the branch.

The desperate spell worked. The branch was pushed away, but not to safety. It fell instead towards Jasper, who had no time to stop it. A moment later she lay motionless underneath the branch.

It had all happened so fast. Uffington could see by the way the branch began to move again that Elizabeth was there, trying to free Jasper. Elizabeth managed to place a hand on Jasper's chest. It was warm but she couldn't feel her heart beating. She tried to find a pulse in her neck but gave up in frustration. Uffington hurried over to the scene. Elizabeth was panicking.

"I don't know what to do. This branch is too heavy to move. We've got to help her."

The consequences—for the Unfortunate Forest as well as Elizabeth's condition—if Jasper died, were too awful to contemplate. Uffington was about to try another spell to remove the branch when she looked up to see one of the Beasts standing by the palace. It watched, its skeletal features twisting as it realised what had happened. Clasping both hands to its throat, it began a howl that bounced off every tree. The sound had nearly faded away when it was taken up by the rest of the Beasts; a dreadful cacophony that came from every corner of the forest.

What was felt by one Beast was felt by all the Beasts.

"They'll be here soon. All of them," said Uffington. "And they'll think it was our fault." She grabbed air a few times before finding Elizabeth. "We must leave."

Elizabeth struggled. "Jasper's my only hope. We've got to stay."

"Jasper might be dead. If they get hold of us we'll wish we were, too. But if she's not, I'll bring you back here myself. Now move."

To leave the Ashen Queen like this was cruel but Uffington was right; the Beasts would be inconsolable, whatever Jasper's condition.

The Beast took a few steps towards them, then began screaming again. This would be their best chance. A slipway led up to the Avenue from the palace. Uffington was aware that her days of running were well behind her and settled for a fast walk. Elizabeth pulled her along. Once up on the Avenue they turned back to glance at Jasper. Beasts were stumbling, crawling, skipping to her. The howls and shrieks were deafening. Muttering a prayer that they would be capable of helping their queen, Uffington cantered along the Avenue. As before, it was a calm route through a forest that was darker and more threatening than ever. As they sighted the path out of the forest, the sound of the Beasts became louder.

"They're after us now for sure," gasped Uffington.

"Where are we going?" asked Elizabeth.

"Back to the caravan. It has all sorts of protection around it."

Would her herbs, rituals and laying down of salt be enough? Nothing untoward had entered the caravan all these years. It was by far their best hope.

Elizabeth's relief at reaching the caravan was countered when she saw how flimsy the door lock was, how easily an exhausted Uffington could fling the door open. The whole structure could be torn open by someone determined enough.

It took Uffington some time to recover. She did not believe in going at anything other than her own pace, but this had been an emergency. It was silent, both inside and outside the caravan. And bitterly cold. After some time had passed, she felt safe enough to make tea. As they sat and drank, all without speaking, they became aware of being watched.

There were faces at every window. The Beasts were peering in. The roof creaked — others were crawling over the caravan, then. The faces had mouths open in screams but were silent. The protection appeared to be working.

Darkness fell. Uffington had walked around the caravan and drawn the curtains. Neither of them would sleep but there was no need to have the Beasts staring at them. They curled up on the small double bed for comfort and warmth.

Something had happened during the night.

To their surprise the women had slept soundly. Uffington shuffled back from the bathroom and cautiously inched the bedroom curtain open.

There was no face at the window.

She turned to the bed. Elizabeth was sitting up; Uffington could see her.

She was faint, like a drifting signal from an old television set. But she had an outline.

"Good morning, Elizabeth," she gasped. "And it is a good morning. There are no Beasts at the window — and I can just about see you."

Elizabeth scrabbled out of bed, to the full length mirror on the wardrobe.

There she was. She was, in truth, barely visible, but when she waved at the mirror, she saw movement waving back. She was scarcely there, but had never looked so beautiful.

They opened all the curtains, expecting to find a terrible face pressed against each window, but there was nothing.

"I wonder if this means the Unfortunate Forest has disappeared?" mused Uffington.

"What about the Ashen Queen? How will we get back to her?" Elizabeth was close to panic again.

"I don't know. The fact that you're partly visible may mean she's alive and is helping you, even from a distance."

Why she would do that after being injured was something neither of them wanted to think about; the price for her help would have certainly increased.

Finally, Uffington opened the caravan door and looked around. The orchard had returned and the Unfortunate Forest had gone. Uffington asked Elizabeth what she wanted to do now. There was only one option.

"I have to go home. I have to see Middlesex Road and Daniel. I won't really believe he's there and safe until I see him."

Uffington closed the door again. "Yes, you need to see him and your neighbours. But you can't tell anyone about what we saw in the forest. It could be disastrous if they re-connected with the Air Leth."

She'd heard of such things happening. What the result was she did not know, but the damage done to the Air Leth in the Unfortunate Forest was catastrophic. In Uffington's opinion, they were unsaveable. Perhaps she should return to the forest alone. Saving Elizabeth was as much as anyone could hope to do now.

Jasper took a short, shallow breath. The pain was intense and she wanted to fill her lungs, to feel properly alive but it wasn't possible, not yet. But she *was* alive; it would take more than a branch flung aside by an inept witch to kill her.

After all their howling and bony hand-wringing, the Beasts had lifted the branch off the Ashen Queen and carried her to the palace. On regaining consciousness she had known immediately that several ribs were broken, but her life was not in danger. It was simply pain she had to deal with; a matter of re-focussing one's energies.

Jasper, born in an active volcano on the Mountain of Vagaries more than half a century ago, had taken her first breath surrounded by molten lava dropping around her like the boiling shit of the Devil. Her skin had adopted the silvery hue of the dust that had covered her at birth; thus the Ashen Queen was named. She had died a thousand times, it seemed, since then, but had made her way back each time. A few broken ribs would do no more than slow her down a little. It wouldn't stop her from getting Elizabeth Longbarrow, the faded woman, back.

The Beasts were not fit to take into Elizabeth's world but they were still useful. The Ashen Queen made them kneel around the biggest of the bog-pools in order to see visions of the witch's hiding place. The vision appeared: the way was open. The Ashen Queen sat on her reassembled travel chair surrounded by new followers—a handful of staggering Air Leth—and made her way towards Enfield.

It had been decided that Elizabeth would visit Middlesex Road while Uffington would rest at home. In reality, as soon as Elizabeth had gone, Uffington had grabbed the shew-stone and gazed at it. She was desperate to see the Unfortunate Forest, to be able to return there as soon as possible. If the Ashen Queen was alive Uffington would beg her for Elizabeth's freedom. Uffington would meet whatever payment was demanded.

But she saw nothing. Her desperation was obscuring her vision. Try as she might, she was unable to clear her mind. It was an immense shock, then, when she looked out of the back window and found the Unfortunate Forest had reappeared and almost had the caravan in its grasp.

She hurried outside, stick in hand, ready to make her way to the palace and face whatever had happened. But there was no need; she spied movement amongst the trees. The Ashen Queen was coming to her.

Middlesex Road was still standing. Elizabeth paused to take in the view of ordinariness before making her way along. Uffington's caravan was less than three miles away but it had taken an age to get here. She had hope now that the horrors of the Unfortunate Forest were unconnected to life here and she was thankful for it. To see Daniel—even if he could not see her—would make whatever was coming next easier to bear.

Everything seemed as it should. The Andersons were getting into their car, a postwoman was delivering letters. Daniel may have already left for work but there would be evidence of his presence inside the house. She knew Uffington would say he didn't deserve her worry, and if he was safe she might vent her fury at the way he let her disappear without a fight, but he didn't deserve what was happening in the forest.

Home, too, looked normal. Safe. Elizabeth nearly cried, sad for the life she'd lost. She'd taken nothing with her when she left except her house keys and was relieved to find them still in her pocket. Once inside she was immediately aware of footsteps upstairs. Daniel was in. She saw movement nearby; a hint of her own reflection in the hall mirror. Overjoyed, she turned to face herself, a small indulgence before she saw Daniel.

But the ghostly image in the mirror was not her own. She reached out and touched the mirror and the reflection did the same. She put her face close to the mirror. To her dismay it was indeed herself she was looking at; faintly visible but different, changed, from when she had faded from sight. The new Elizabeth Longbarrow was shorter, darker, perhaps South American. How had such a change occurred? Who was she now? Uffington had no reason to do such a thing (and Elizabeth didn't think her capable). It had to have happened in the Unfortunate Forest.

Daniel was suddenly making his way down the stairs towards her. This was truly her husband, not the tortured creature in the forest.

While with Uffington she had learnt to project her voice and she did so now.

"Daniel! It's me. It's Elizabeth."

Is it? She wondered.

He stopped, inches from her, aware of something nearby but not knowing what it was. She waved her arms up and down right in front of his face.

Daniel frowned.

He heard a voice he thought he remembered, but it was just his mind playing tricks. There was no one there.

Uffington knew they had not left the forest to find her but she hurried to meet them anyway. She was delighted to see the Ashen Queen. Jasper was sitting upright in her wriggling travel chair, her face taut with pain. She motioned for the chair and followers to stop and she let Uffington approach.

"That was an inept attempt at murder," said the Ashen Queen coldly.

"Your Mercifulness, it was an accident." Uffington blustered her apologies and begged forgiveness. "We came to you to ask for help. The last thing I wanted was to hurt you."

"I see no sign of Elizabeth. Where is she?" Jasper was amused at the witch's discomfort but it was time to get to business.

Uffington looked around at the dozen or so poor souls who accompanied the Ashen Queen. They were bewildered at their freedom, shocked at their own appalling injuries. Who knew how long they'd existed, what life they'd led, before the Beasts had got to them?

"Please, please don't take the Air Leth with you. Let them wait for you here," she begged.

The Ashen Queen smiled again. "The Air Leth will meet their other selves. That is my price for making Elizabeth Longbarrow visible."

The termite chair moved on. Uffington grabbed at the nearest of the entourage, letting go of his mauled arm when it threatened to come off in her hand. The man turned to her, close to death from exhaustion. He mouthed something she could not decipher and got back into step with the others.

There was nothing Uffington could do except follow.

Outside, in the sunshine, Elizabeth was easier to see. Daniel knew he had heard her voice this time, but the ghost in front of him was not his wife. Elizabeth tried again, distraught to see that his expression was one of confusion rather than recognition.

There was so much she wanted to say to him.

Daniel, incapable of acknowledging what was in front of him, was about to head for his car when he noticed that most of his neighbours were standing outside their homes, gawping at some unseen thing coming up the road.

There it was—a figure on a dark, moving chair, at its sides the survivors of a disaster. Except that they were mirror images of his neighbours standing on the pavement. And they were headed by a perverse copy of himself.

Elizabeth saw them but she was so excited at the sight of Jasper that she hardly noticed who was in the crowd. Uffington was pleading with the Ashen Queen, presumably to keep her wounded entourage away from Middlesex Road. She shouted to Daniel that he should go back inside the house and ran down to the Ashen Queen. Jasper, seeing her faint outline, ordered the chair to stop again. She waved aside Elizabeth's gushing relief at her re-appearance.

"You took my hand in the palace. And now you're partly visible. You must return to the Unfortunate Forest with me to complete your healing."

"Why have you brought these... people with you?" asked Elizabeth, refusing to look any of them in the eye, but seeing that her husband's double was amongst them.

Uffington answered. "They're the price! The Ashen Queen wants to see what'll happen when both selves meet."

"There must be something else you want?" pleaded Elizabeth.

The Ashen Queen looked down at her, her features set in stone.

"Air Leth are created before birth, during birth, at various points during a person's life," she said. "Most are too busy sleepwalking to realise it has happened. Don't you want to see how they'll react to each other? What they'll do to each other? To see such a thing, to learn; what more could I want? Besides," she continued dryly, "you might prefer your Air Leth husband."

Mr and Mrs Anderson were now face to face with the versions of themselves that had been freed from the grip of the Beasts. John Anderson was in by far the worst condition.

Blood oozed from the places pierced by the Beast. Amy Anderson, crucified on the banisters of her staircase, could only stagger up to the perfect looking woman who had discarded her so long ago and gaze into her eyes.

Elizabeth faced the Ashen Queen again.

"If this is the cost then I'll stay as I am. Take them back."

"And return them to the Beasts? You're quick to forget," the Ashen Queen replied, watching with great interest. The Air Leth couple stretched their injured arms to the sky. In a sudden movement they yanked the Andersons' mouths open and climbed inside, swelling their hosts' throats as they made their way down.

Mr and Mrs Anderson, motionless throughout the process, came to as soon as it was over. They turned to each other and embraced desperately, as if they'd had news of a terrible tragedy, then helped one another into their home.

The rest of the Air Leth began to limp towards their other bodies. Uffington gazed sadly at the Andersons' house.

"They look haunted. Is that what the Air Leth really are: ghosts?"

Jasper was nodding. "Ghosts of a kind," she said. "All your nightmares, your fears, your unhappiness. All the things you couldn't bear to remember or experience, torn away to become another self, another soul. And now; all of those things, returned."

Daniel Longbarrow, still standing by his car at the far end of the road, watched the events unfold. As his mirror image hobbled towards him he vomited onto his shoes.

Elizabeth begged the Ashen Queen for mercy.

"I'll come with you, I'll do anything. Just keep that thing away from my husband."

"You're coming with me anyway. We made a contract and the price has to be paid. It might do your husband good to re-join his Air Leth self."

Elizabeth turned to Uffington, who reluctantly shook her head.

"It's beyond my power to do anything. And I've already done so much damage. The only comfort I can offer is that many of your neighbours should be able to console each other. Your husband will be in sympathetic company."

Elizabeth climbed onto the travel chair.

"I'll come back," she shouted to Daniel. "As soon as I'm healed. I'll be back to help you."

The Ashen Queen smiled. "I'll take you to the Mountain of Vagaries, I'll show you all the wonders of the forest. You'll have no time for *here* after that."

Uffington silently agreed. Part of her envied the experiences Elizabeth would have with the Ashen Queen but she also feared for her friend. And she wondered about her partial re-appearance; was it the Ashen Queen's doing that Elizabeth kept looking at her hands and arms as if she didn't recognise them as her own? Who, exactly, was she returning as?

Uffington said nothing of her misgivings as she accompanied the pair back to her caravan. Instead she offered Elizabeth words of encouragement for what lay ahead, knowing that she was going to encounter things that Uffington had had only the briefest glimpses of during what now seemed a very sheltered lifetime of charms, visions and magic.

When they got to the caravan she gave the most casual *au revoir* she could muster. She unlocked the door and lingered there, watching the strange sight of the Ashen Queen on her termite chair, the hint of a figure riding behind, as they disappeared amongst the trees. By morning the Unfortunate Forest had disappeared, too. In its place stood the apple trees and the peaceful fields again.

One day, Uffington knew, she would use the shew-stone and would find the Unfortunate Forest again and, perhaps, Elizabeth Longbarrow.

Whoever she might have become.

The Man who Builds the Ruins

"This," he said, "is a lovely place to be lost in."

And they *were* lost. To an extent, anyway, easily rectifiable with a bit of compass and map-work. They—Esteban and his partner, Paco—had come to the Basque Forest to be away from the crowds of Madrid. It was good to be off the beaten track, crossing shallow streams and kicking through the fallen autumn leaves. Paco grabbed him and they laughed, the only human voices in the world.

When they came across the building, it was a shock to the senses. It was a vast structure, in a state of complete ruin. After staring open-mouthed at it for some time the pair climbed over what was once a wall and tried to take it in. Moss lay on the scattered stones, trees grew through the cracked stone floor; nature was gladly reclaiming it. The immense building, shaped like a cross, was beautiful to behold, despite its condition.

Esteban looked at the map and shook his head. "I know where we are now. This isn't marked. There was no mention of this on the website. It looks like a church. How can it be here?"

Paco managed to get a signal on his phone

and did a quick search. "It comes up with nothing. Someone must know it's here." He looked over the ruins again. His eyes widened and he put his phone away. "I think I've seen this place before," he whispered. "But... it can't be. I've been in this building, but not here." He ran across the inside of the building and out of a doorway, yelling for Esteban when he got there.

The remains of a gigantic dome were scattered across the forest floor. It confirmed what Paco suspected, bizarre at it was.

"Do you remember," he said, as Esteban joined him, "when we were in London? You worked for a couple of days and I went sightseeing. I spent a whole day in this place."

Esteban frowned, not understanding. Paco spelt it out.

"This building," he gasped, "is the greatest in London. It's not a church, it's more than that. This is St Paul's Cathedral."

She had wanted to keep the magazine away from him, but he found it in the recycling bag and was reading the article on himself before she could stop him.

"Why is it that Raymond Belarius, who so lovingly designs contemporary yet warm and, above all, homely homes, restricts himself to glass and steel when he creates buildings and offices? It is as if he is punishing the worker by making them work in such ruins of design; perhaps to send them home, grateful to have survived the workday and ever more appreciative of where his real talents lay — despite not being able to afford one of his homes."

There was more but Louisa grabbed the

magazine and Raymond made no attempt to stop her.

"You shouldn't read anything about your-self," she chided him. "It only hurts you."

Raymond held up his hands. "I usually don't. I saw my name on the cover and couldn't help myself." He smiled at his sister, but was not forgiven.

"You're a brilliant architect. You and I and a million others know it. But journalists! It's their job to misunderstand you. Perhaps, if you were not so honest... "

She was right. His most famous quote, also his most ridiculed, was that he dreamt of architecture, that the designs of his buildings came to him in dreams. It had brought him legions of fans in Europe—where much of his work was situated—but derision in Britain. It was construed as being a little too close to acknowledging his own talent, to portraying himself as a visionary. For Raymond, it was simply a part of the process, if anything a confession that his ideas came from elsewhere, but the quote was widely misinterpreted. It did not affect his work but he had become more cautious, almost reclusive, in his private life. Louisa worried about him. Her brother was the rich, famous one and yet she, happy with her husband and two children, was surely the better off. He did not express any feelings of loneliness, seemed to have no wish for a partner, but over recent years had, she suspected, begun to suffer from depression. He would sometimes give a deep sigh. When one of her daughters had asked him why he did it, he had replied, *"The beauty of life is sometimes eclipsed by its sadness"*, but had never elaborated.

But he was in demand, for public and private buildings, and that seemed to make him happy. He was making his own, distinct mark on the world and he loved that he could travel to cities as far apart as Reykjavik and Naples and see his work, functioning and appreciated. Perhaps that was why the magazine article, far from hurting him, only appeared to amuse him. Louisa was relieved. Perspective was needed in these things.

Raymond was in his office when news of the discovery in the Basque Forest broke. His PA caught his eye. She was looking out of the window, bending into awkward shapes to try and see around the neighbouring buildings.

It was distracting. Raymond opened his door. "Jo, what the devil are you doing?"

"Sorry, I'm just trying to see if St Paul's is still there."

She relaxed, having spied the dome, and explained her baffling reply.

"Apparently St Paul's Cathedral has been found in the north of Spain. Bits of it, anyway. The couple who found it thought the Cathedral had been picked up from London and dropped into a forest. I've seen footage. It looks exactly like St Paul's—if the place had been bombed. An exact copy. How's that possible?"

It sounded like a hoax. Raymond told her to get on, but later on he looked up the story. It was, in fact, an extraordinary event. The authorities responsible for the Basque Forest had no idea the place contained such a building, which seemed implausible—the building had not been uncovered, it was merely *there*, as if it had been built hundreds of years ago and left to fall apart. One of the hikers who'd discovered it described it as a 'miracle'. It was located in a quiet area of the forest, but one that was open to walkers, yet no one had any notion that it had ever been there. The forest authorities were investigating. The popular theory was that Sir Christopher Wren had built this copy, for whatever reason, when he'd built St Paul's, and it had fallen into ruin soon afterwards, judging by the vegetation growing through and around it.

Raymond frowned. Why would Wren do such a thing? The work required to construct two such magnificent buildings was phenomenal. And to leave one to neglect as soon as it was finished, in the middle of nowhere, was utter nonsense. Wren wouldn't have wasted his time. It was probably a lot of hysteria—it would turn out to be an art installation of some kind, a poor copy of part of the cathedral, with the story hyped out of all proportion. He worked late, looking at the preliminary plans for what was already being described as 'the ultimate Belarius home'; a new home for the ultra-wealthy Mendelssohn family, to be built on the banks of the Thames at Wapping in place of a demolished wharf. He could retire after this one, if he wanted. But there was something about it that grated. The plans just didn't sit right. Eventually he left them be. It would come to him. It always did.

After he'd finished for the day, he went for a drink. The Lamb was a gloriously old-fashioned pub and remained comfortably undiscovered by tourists despite its central location. His face was well known, both as a local and for his celebrity, but he was always treated with quiet respect. Sat in a corner, he mused over the day. A flicker of an idea was coming to him. Later, as he walked home to Albermarle Way, he found himself sighing. *The sadness*, as he called it, was creeping up on him again. As was often the case, he had no idea what had triggered it. But this time, instead of threatening to swallow him, it goaded him into action.

And so the next afternoon he was standing in the Basque Forest, trying to take in the incredible ruins of St Paul's Cathedral. He had called Jo from the airport that morning and she had protested strongly; Suzanne Mendelssohn was expecting to talk to him that day. Raymond had replied that the Mendelssohns could wait. And he knew they *would* wait; his reputation trumped their wealth. He had not been able to stop thinking of the outrageous discovery in Spain and whatever the reason for it being there—an insane duplicate by Wren, art project or whatever else it turned out to be—the fine workmanship that he'd seen on the news was something he wanted to see first hand. And now he was here it was even more breath-taking. The forest authorities were still examining the ruins, taking photographs and measurements. The general public were being kept away, but Raymond Belarius was not the general public. One of the archaeologists, a woman half his age, had given him a hard hat and taken him around the building, pointing out the details of the remaining work. Raymond asked if there were any more theories on the building's origins.

"Estimating the age of the trees growing through the floor, I would say this place was built early in the eighteenth century," she said, in English that put his Spanish to shame, "and quickly fell into ruin, although why that happened is a mystery. Some of the masonry has been taken for analysis. We hope to have more answers soon."

"I just don't see why Wren would have done such a thing," said Raymond. "Or who else would copy him while St Paul's was being built. Is there any evidence of it being used for worship?"

"Not yet," said the woman. "But if you give me your email address, I can keep you updated on all developments."

He gave her his card and thanked her.

"It was a pleasure to meet you, Señor Belarius," she said, and left him to it.

Now he could explore in detail and he made a thorough investigation, taking photographs but at times just breathing the place in. He stood inside the remains, almost dizzy at the sight of the tallest remaining wall, its glassless window looming over him, framing the trees outside. He stood by the broken dome, moved almost to tears at the ruin of such a monumental work. Now he was here the damage was clearly far older than the wayward Second World War bomb he had been imagining had caused the destruction.

He stayed at the site until dusk, then returned to his hotel. The trip had done him good, despite the ruin's unanswered questions. An afternoon flight to London tomorrow would have him back in discussions with the Mendlessohns by the end of the week.

The hotel bar was quiet, the beer cool and drinkable. Raymond was on his third, and last, of the evening, when he noticed the man at the bar. He looked thoughtful, his prominent cheekbones and narrow chin giving his face a triangular appearance. The man caught his gaze and walked over, his movement mannered and effeminate. Raymond silently cursed; his curiosity had no doubt been misinterpreted. The man asked if he could join Raymond for a short time.

"I can shed some light on the beautiful building you saw today," he said, his accent heavy.

Was he Spanish? Mexican? How did he know where Raymond had been? Did he work for the forest authority? The man smiled.

"Señor Belarius, a great architect does not come to this small town without good reason. Why else would you be here? But I must introduce myself. My name is Señor Raoul."

He offered his hand. Raymond shook it. The man was, at least, interested in architecture. They discussed the ruins.

"Incredible work," said Raymond. "Too skilled to be anyone but Wren, even as a copy. But why waste all that time, that skill? The man was sane as far as I know."

Raoul sat back, beer in hand.

"What would you say if I told you the building was completed less than five years ago?"

Raymond laughed. "It'd be a shoddy job, then, to have fallen into ruin in that time. And it wouldn't be possible—those trees growing through the floor must be at least a century old. What on Earth makes you think it's that recent?"

"Because I built it, Señor Belarius."

Of course. Every attention seeker and lunatic in Spain would be claiming the same thing. Raymond finished his beer and got up.

"Well, you're a terrible architect and a worse stonemason. Good night to you."

He made his way to his room, had his door almost closed when a voice hissed from the corridor."

"Señor Belarius! Let me explain."

Raymond was about to shut the door in Raoul's face, but the thought of him lurking outside was unpleasant. He would face him and give the man a bloody nose if need be; better to sort it out right now.

"Please leave," he ordered, "or I'll have to break my rule about not resorting to violence."

"Señor Belarius, I built St Paul's Cathedral as a ruin because I saw it as a ruin. It is the building's fate."

Raymond had closed the door but, hearing Raoul's claim, re-opened it.

"Why should I believe you have anything to do with the building?"

In reply, Raoul held up his hands. He was a slight man, well-educated judging by the way he dressed and spoke, but his hands were not those of a middle-class professional. They were dark and weathered like his face but where his face looked healthy his hands were battered and worn, almost to the point of deformity. The hands of a lifelong stonemason or builder. As evidence went, it wasn't much. And yet Raymond was intrigued.

They sat in his room and Raoul spoke.

"Just as you see your finished projects in dreams, Señor, I see the ruins that a building will become. In dreams, awake, at any time. I was in London and people were queuing to go into St Paul's and all I could see was them walking into a ruined building. This was several years ago. I dreamt the ruins again and again and I drew plans of what I saw. Down to the moss on the stones, the trees breaking through the beautiful floor. Do you understand the undertaking? The compulsion? I *had* to make the building—and the moss, and the trees. There was no choice. I'm an architect, as you are, Señor Belarius. You create monuments to the present. I build monuments to the future."

Raymond found he was enjoying the conversation. The man seemed harmless and this hypothetical debate was probably all he needed. He gestured for Raoul to continue.

"Destruction and decay are to be as celebrated as creation and growth. My buildings are as glorious as yours—as are the originals— because the future is as glorious as the present and the past."

"So, if the ruin is St Paul's future, when will it happen?" he asked. Raoul looked grim.

"I do not know, but it will be sooner than you think. *The End* is always sooner than we dare to think. I did not mean for the ruin to be discovered, I thought it well hidden. The others will be safe, I hope. They are my burden; no one else's."

There were more? The man's delusion knew no bounds. He talked at length of ruins scattered around the world, hidden in forests or buried, away from human eyes. In Chile he had built and buried an American shopping mall, in the north of Finland was a suburban Parisian street submerged in a deep lake. The list went on. He even claimed to have built the remains of an Egyptian Pyramid, hidden in a Russian forest.

"Do not misunderstand me," he concluded. "I am proud of my work. Every detail, you will agree, is faithful to the original. I have been doing this for such a long time, Señor Belarius. I hope you can appreciate my efforts. Your buildings are full of life, they are functional and beautiful. Mine are like cemeteries in comparison. But they are necessary. It is important to acknowledge Fate, what Time has in store for us, however frightening it might be."

When Raoul had gone, without protest once his story was told, Raymond went straight to bed. The sketches that his visitor had left him — rough maps showing where his other projects were, each marked CONFIDENTIAL — lay on the desk, bound for the waste bin when he checked out.

Suzanne Mendlessohn was quite clear about what she wanted in a home. After setting it out at length, she took a photograph out of her bag. It was a family portrait.

"This is the most important thing, Mr Belarius. It's going to be our home. I don't want a showpiece, I want somewhere we'll look forward to coming home to."

She left him the photograph and he stuck

it to his computer screen. Five faces smiled out at him like a ray of light. This was what he'd been waiting for. The woman was a genius, he thought joyfully, and he studied the plans with a new enthusiasm for the project.

Within a week the dream, the vision, of the place came to him. It was wonderful; a country home made for twenty-first century urban living. There was space and light, but not so much as to detract from it being a family home. There was room for privacy without it turning to isolation. Raymond spent long hours in his studio at Albermarle Way, perfecting the plans.

It was during this time that he came across the maps Raoul had given him. He must have decided not to throw them away after all. He had not spared the man much thought since arriving back in London. There had been no time for such things, but now he remembered their conversation and looked over the sketches. If Raoul believed his own claims, then he had a sad life. To see the world only in terms of its destruction must be unbearable. Raymond had his own demons; a habit of lingering over the worst pieces of news, a need to be aware of how bad many people's lives were. To balance this, perhaps, his work was all about creation. As for Raoul, his *monuments to the future* were surely just signposts to the end of civilisation. He claimed there was beauty in the ruin of St Paul's Cathedral, but it was just decay, a corpse of a building. It was a lonely delusion.

Raymond began to dream of ruins.

During the daytime he refined his drawings of the Mendlessohn house and worked on the model. He was tempted to think it might be his greatest work. Each night, however, he returned to the Basque Forest and was overwhelmed again by the remains of St Paul's. He dreamt of other places; one night he was underwater in a freezing Finnish lake, somehow walking along a street, the red-tiled roofs of the houses collapsed in on themselves, the windows smashed, the doors hanging off their hinges. The next night he was in a Buddhist temple that lay, almost buried, in the sands of Tunisia, the inside of the building ravaged by fire.

It was in the temple that he met Raoul again.

Louisa had pressed the bell a hundred times before Raymond let her in. Despite his smile, he looked worse than she thought he would.

"You were supposed to come over last night," she said. "I left messages on your landline and your mobile. Why didn't you let me know you couldn't come? Are you alright?"

"I'm fine. Actually, I'm very good, just wrapped up in a project," he said, checking his phones, surprised to find messages. "Sorry for not calling. It slipped my mind. I don't usually miss your meals."

"When was the last time you ate?"

He shrugged.

"Good job I bought your dinner, then," she said, holding up a carrier bag, and made for the kitchen. She could hear him sighing, but it sounded more like exhaustion than melancholy.

She called out that his food would be ready in a few minutes, then took the opportunity to have a look around his studio. It was no secret that he was designing the Mendlessohn home. He didn't discuss work much with her. She wished he did. People too rich or important to live in ordinary houses were the subject of ridicule in her household, but her brother's inspiration was of continual interest to her.

She cast her eye over the drawings of the house then caught sight of the model of the building and went for a closer look.

What she saw had her hurrying back to her brother.

She let him eat before asking again if he was alright.

"I went to the studio. You're having trouble with the Mendlessohn house."

He looked surprised. "It's going very well, actually."

"The model... it looks like a smashed toy. This is why you need to eat occasionally."

Again the quizzical look.

"The model's perfect."

They went down to the studio.

The Mendlessohn house was a ruin in miniature. Raymond's perfect model was, at first glance, utterly wrecked. Then he realised that it had not been smashed in frustration but *created* as a wreckage, with skill. They searched the three floors of Raymond's flat but there was no sign of a break-in or of Raoul. Raymond told his sister about his trip to Spain and the meeting with the man who was claiming to have built the ruined copy of St Paul's.

"The strange thing was," he said, "when

we were talking, he sounded completely rational. It could almost have been true."

Louisa looked to the heavens.

"Delusional people aren't always ranting and raving. I heard the copy had turned out to be centuries old. You couldn't keep a project like that secret in this day and age."

Raymond gazed out of the window to the nearby graveyard.

"Perhaps no one found it because no one was looking for it," he said.

The temple was at the bottom of the sand dune. He was tired so he half fell onto the hot sand and slid down. He had never been inside a Buddhist temple but, like St Paul's, even the catastrophic damage had not extinguished its effect. The huge statue of the reclining Buddha was almost untouched, gleaming gold and dazzling in the sun's reflection. Everywhere that wasn't covered in sand or destroyed by fire was a riot of colour.

Raymond knew he was dreaming, but the heat of the sand, the smell of burnt wood, had the clarity of waking life.

Raoul appeared. He ran his hand over the charred remains of a statue then brushed his hand clean. He wore a flowing white robe in the heat and as he approached Raymond, the tattoos on his legs—strange diagrams and symbols, a man with the head of a goat—were clearly visible.

Raymond admonished him. "You broke into my home and swapped the Mendlessohn model!"

"You needed to see it."

"A sick joke," spat Raymond. "As all your

buildings are."

Anger flashed across Raoul's face. "These buildings are a lifetime's work," he said. "They are no less important than yours. This temple," he swept his hand around him, "has been a sacred place for longer than either of us can imagine. Its ruin does not make it less so, Señor. As stones and mortar, it is temporary. As all things are. But what it symbolises cannot be destroyed by fire. I built this ruin with reverence, as you no doubt do your work. But for the first time I have seen a vision of a ruin that I knew was not yet built; the Mendlessohn home will be a disaster. Do not build it."

The dream dissolved and Raymond fell into deep sleep, sweating from the desert heat.

Of all the ruins he'd built, it was the Egyptian Pyramid that gave Raoul the most pleasure. He had worked on more beautiful buildings and more complicated projects (the street under water had been especially so), but the Pyramid gave him the most hope. It was many thousands of years old, yet it was still almost complete, would be so until the Earth was incinerated by the Sun. It was on the inside that the ruin presented itself. Excavation—looting by respectable men— had deprived it of its riches and diminished its influence. But the fact that it was still almost intact far into the future was surely a sign for optimism. It looked out of place in the forest, its yellow limestone blocks at odds with the trees, although the winter snow was easily capable of making it disappear into the landscape.

The process of building had been the same

as the others. After the dreams and visions that had provided him with the technical drawings, he had travelled to central Russia and, with great difficulty, had found the area of forest he was looking for. He had set up his basic camp and then had taken the scrying mirror from his bag. It was prehistoric, made of bronze, the front highly polished to give a reflection. The back of the mirror was exquisitely decorated, as was befitting its original owner.

Raoul sat and stared into the mirror. The magical transmitter. The magical *receiver*. Unblinking, his breathing almost stopped, he passed into a trance state.

At some unknown stage during the day—time had moved forwards, backwards and sideways—his assistants had appeared from the gloom of the trees and set about making the stones for Raoul to dress.

Exactly where (or when) the assistants came from, what they were, Raoul didn't know, but they appeared whenever he used the scrying mirror. They were outlandish creatures, reminiscent of the Chimera of ancient Greek mythology. Their human bodies only began from the shoulders down; they had the heads and necks of goats.

Their ridged horns curled up, away from their heads, thick beards hung below their long, strong faces. Male and female, there appeared to be no hierarchy. They would study the plans with their dead-looking goat eyes, bleat orders at one another and create whatever was needed, using their own bodily fluids and waste. A magical process transformed and aged it into the appropriate tools and materials but Raoul was not permitted to see it. All he knew was that the assistants were intelligent, skilled workers, as many as were required for each job. And each one was stronger than ten men. Raoul had at first tried to match them but had soon given up.

But he worked, oh he worked. It showed in his damaged hands and weary demeanour. But the work was a privilege to do. He ended each day of it in tears of exhaustion and rapture.

Much as Raoul had not meant for any of his work to be discovered, the reaction to the ruins of St Paul's had been pleasing. Amongst the confusion was deep emotion and appreciation, and the general opinion was still that this was a lost work of Sir Christopher Wren's. This suited Raoul—no one would suspect that more existed—but there was now the temptation to vanity, to announce the truth to the world. In speaking to Raymond Belarius he had succumbed to that temptation. He had believed this until he'd had the vision of the Mendlessohn house. Now he saw the purpose of breaking his silence. He supposed that, in ordinary circumstances, he might have been elated at a vision of an as yet unbuilt building. It should have been a wonderful moment.

And it would have been; had it not been for all the blood.

His first job was to find his own, complete model of the Mendlessohn project. Raymond searched the studio, hoping that Raoul had not taken or destroyed it. To his relief he found it, placed carefully in an empty drawer of the filing cabinet.

It had not been damaged.

He almost swiped the ruined version off the table but a glint inside the building caught his eye. He looked at the ruin in detail for the first time.

The model was elaborate, a perfect reproduction of his plans. Raoul was a skilled madman, if nothing else. But apart from the wreckage itself something else, inside the building, sent a chill through his bones.

The main reception room was covered in blood. Pools glimmered on the floor, thick streaks lined the walls. A sticky mass in the centre of the room contained a tiny hand and arm, torn off at the elbow, in intricate and appalling detail.

Raymond spied down upon the scene through the smashed roof and upper floor, a gigantic interloper in a tragedy. It was undoubtedly a threat. Raymond's instinct told him that Raoul was not a violent man but the model suggested otherwise. If he saw the man again—in real life as opposed to in a dream— then he'd call the police. There didn't appear to be any other choice.

The weeks went by and Raoul was not seen or heard of, much to Raymond's relief. The story of Northern Spain's version of St Paul's Cathedral faded into the background. The plans for the Mendlessohn house were approved, the foundations laid. Still wary of Raoul, however, Raymond had the site surrounded by high wooden fences. Since officially it was to keep the press out, it intensified speculation as to the kind of building Belarius had planned. He was known for being strikingly ambitious rather than outrageous for the sake of publicity; people wondered whether this could be a change of direction. Raymond ignored it all; as usual, the finished building, the years of happiness the Mendlessohns would have in it, would speak for itself.

Life settled back into its normal, busy routine. Raymond still dreamt of ruined buildings, but the dreams were less vivid. Raoul appeared only once—lying, still, on a bed in a sparsely furnished room. Louisa expressed relief that her brother was in better health and made Raymond promise that he would not let work get on top of him again. Spain had drifted from Raymond's mind so much that he was surprised when the email from Imelda Espina, the archaeologist who had shown him around the Basque site, appeared in his Inbox. He was still interested in her findings, however, and opened the email immediately. Analysis of various pieces of masonry from the Basque Forest site, she said, were proving contradictory. Whilst most of it appeared to have been worked in the late 17th Century, one piece, to all appearances like the rest, was made of an unknown material that had been worked far more recently—during the 20th Century. No one had any theories as to how this could be the case; more analysis had to be done. Imelda was clearly fascinated by the strange masonry sample. Tests showed that the material was 'almost' stone—as if was on its way to becoming the same stone as the rest of the building but hadn't quite got there. And how the recently worked block could be in the middle of such an old wall—and fixed there with old mortar—was incomprehensible.

In the light of what Raoul had said, the information was disconcerting, but it did not stop Raymond from having a particularly productive day and he stayed on at the site to have a look around when everyone else had left. Progress was indeed good; the house was beginning to rise from the ground, a Thing being dragged into creation, hinting at what it would become. Satisfied, he was about to leave when he became aware that someone was on the site with him. It was more sensed than heard. He walked quietly through the beginnings of the house again. In what would be the kitchen stood Raoul. He rocked back and forth as if on the brink of collapse. His dark skin was almost pale. He grasped a metal object in his hand. It was bronze, at first glance a valuable antique.

Raymond's hand closed over the phone in his trouser pocket.

"How did you like Tunisia?" asked Raoul. His voice was calm, gentle.

Raymond stopped. He had told no one about the dream. The man was full of tricks, no more than a fairground mystic.

"I'm going to call the police," said Raymond. "I'm going to make sure you stay away this time."

"I'm not here to hurt you or harass you," said Raoul. "I shouldn't have tried to stop you doing your work. It was a moment of weakness. Please forgive me."

"We agree on that, then," said Raymond. "But I can't have you just appearing in my life like this."

He fell silent, aware that he sounded as if he was rejecting a lover.

Raoul looked at him with eyes that were glazed over. His words were slightly slurred, as if he was talking in his sleep.

"You must build this wonderful home. If it does not exist then *my* building cannot exist. There is no future if there is no present. I did not remember that when we met in the temple."

He rocked so far forwards that Raymond was sure he'd fall, but righted himself. A noise came from the main reception room. Raymond took out his phone.

Raoul breathed deeply. "I am near the end of my life. I will die before this house is built."

"I'm still calling the police," snapped Raymond. He wanted this over with.

"Finish this house tonight and I will have time to build my version of it. We will help you."

Raymond's thumb hit 999 and he was about to push the 'dial' key when there was more noise behind him.

And then: bleating.

A huge hand closed around Raymond's and gently took the phone away, then the creature walked over to Raoul and handed it to him. It was extraordinary; at least a foot taller than both men, for the most part a near-naked, pregnant woman.

From the neck up, it was a goat.

Raoul came back to himself, smiled at the assistant and slipped the phone into his pocket. He looked a little better.

"There's no Time like the present," he said.

More assistants appeared, dozens of them,

male and female, ready for the remarkable task ahead. The site took on the smell of a farmyard.

They didn't force Raymond to help. They didn't need to; no one, no *thing*, was going to take over one of his projects. Running away was not an option. Time slowed until it was almost standing still. The goat-people began appearing with bricks, cement, steel joists. Where were the supplies coming from? Raymond peered around a corner and saw, in what would be the front garden, how the creatures were gathering the raw materials needed to make the building equipment.

And 'raw' was the word. They were collecting their own shit and spit. Somehow they were turning it into everything they needed, down to the nails and screws.

The house took shape. When the walls were raised above head height the goat-people stood upon each other's shoulders like a circus act, and passed materials up from the ground. They worked confidently and efficiently. Evidently they knew Raymond's plans inside out.

Raymond worked harder than he'd ever done. Soon he was down to his vest and trousers, his jacket and shirt discarded in a corner despite the chill of the night. He carried bricks, he made window frames, he wired power points and installed plumbing. He had only a basic knowledge of most of these things, but Raoul or one of his assistants directed him. At first he had wanted to stop them, had been biding his time to see if there was a weakness he could exploit despite how outnumbered he was, but as they worked together, their skill and efficiency astonished him. They more than did justice to his plans; the Mendlessohn house was coming to life before his eyes, all the more beautiful for the work of the assistants. He was still afraid of them, although he knew it was unnecessary — they were artists, not soldiers. But the closer he got to them, the stronger the smell was; it was primeval, far more animal than human. It made him nervous. But as time went on he found it becoming less offensive.

In the early hours of the next morning, in the shell of what would be one of the bedrooms, the two humans had a short break. Raymond wiped his face on his vest.

"So, handsome Señor Belarius," said Raoul, "is this not a wonderful thing? Your beautiful house will be completed before daybreak. It will be considered a miracle."

Raymond was too exhausted for niceties.

"How long will it be standing? Before it becomes the ruin you want it to be?"

"I don't know," said Raoul. "I do not dream dates. It could be a matter of years or just a few months. Not long for the life of such a building. It will surely mean death for someone. I do not wish this, it is simply Fate. But I cannot help but be sad. You are familiar with sadness, are you not? You feel it often."

Goat-people joined them, ready to finish work on the bedrooms. Raymond took the opportunity to leave but he wanted the last word. He tried his best to make it defiant.

"This house will stand for generations," he said. "It has to. But you're right — this building will be the most treasured of my career. And no one will ever know how I built it."

He got to the bottom of the staircase before he broke down in tears. It was all too much; the magnificence of the building, the view through the huge window in front of him of the fetid creatures outside, master craftsmen all, working in as close to darkness as London was capable of. And he was exhausted. But still he worked. He picked himself up and worked his way around the building, trying to find a flaw. Everything was perfect, every line level and true. The house was everything he could have wished for.

They finished minutes before daybreak.

Still bare-chested, on hands and knees outside the house, Raymond grunted his thanks as one of the goat-people collected his jacket and wrapped it around him to stop him from freezing. Raoul, also spent, had been hoisted up by a goat-woman and lay gratefully in her arms. She carried him to Raymond and Raoul addressed him in a fading voice.

"Your workmen will be arriving very soon, Señor Belarius. I wonder what you shall tell them? You may not be able to divulge the secret of this house, but you will get full credit for the achievement. It is your masterpiece. Do not drown in the sadness of what it will become; let the future arrive in its own good time."

The curious group gathered together. One of the goat-people helped Raymond up and sat him on the garden wall. Its gentleness, such a contrast to its appearance, almost had Raymond in tears again. It re-joined the others. They all peered at him for a few moments then made their way around the fences and disappeared from sight, leaving Raymond, alone, to watch the dawn illuminate the Mendlessohn's new home for the first time.

March of the Marvellous

It had rained in the far west of Levanthia for most of the night. Low cloud settled over the high ground but on the coast the wind whipped around the cliffs and coves. In the village of Bos'cairn Mor, the inhabitants drifted off to sleep with the sound of the wind rattling the windows and hurling everything that hadn't been completely secured up into the air and around the lanes. They awoke, as one, at first light, when the wind and rain suddenly ceased. The silence was blissful, but short-lived. From far away came what sounded like a hum, so quiet at first that it could be mistaken for a trick of the mind after the din of the storm. Slowly it began to gather strength, and by dawn it was no longer possible to dismiss as imagination. The hum rose and fell, rose and fell. It was a sound with rhythm and tone and form, as different from the anarchy of the night's weather as it was possible to be. The village, a collection of houses at its centre with a few outlying farms, came to life as the inhabitants began, with growing excitement, to fancy what the source of the sound might be. Those who were quickest ready took turns to scour the skyline, hoping to be first to spot the group that it was hoped would pass their way.

As the sun crept up, a woman ran back into the village from her vantage point, perched on top of a jagged finger of rock, and breathlessly gave the news; the March of the Marvellous was approaching.

The Marvellous were markedly different to the rest of the Greater Blood and their lifestyles resembled those of a nomadic, religious people. Every few months they would up sticks and find a new part of Levanthia to make their home. It was their way, they said, of honouring their magical land. They asked for nothing from anyone, and crossed the land with little interaction with others, but on occasion they would accept the hospitality of those they met along the way. Stories of the Marvellous had been told throughout Levanthian history and their presence was welcomed and considered a great blessing. Luck would come to those who witnessed it.

In a country of miracles, the marchers were perhaps the most miraculous of all. They were people who, over generations, had absorbed more of Levanthia's magic than anyone else. Affected in the womb or at birth, born during peculiar weather conditions or other strange happenings, a very different kind of Greater Blood had been created. Unlike Levanthians, who were born with varying degrees of power, the Marvellous— their family names long forgotten in favour of a more celebratory title—had magic running riot through their bodies. It gave them a most bizarre appearance. Arms or legs, or a single appendage, might be several yards long; a head might be twisted or flattened or split in two; some might walk on all fours, or have an extra eye staring out from a torso that could be stick thin or gigantic. They had taken themselves away from the rest of the population by choice long ago, to learn how to safely control and use their differences. In the main they succeeded, and good magic was said to flow from them as they travelled. The group was small, perhaps two dozen adults and young, quite capable of disappearing into cover of any kind, be it rocks, rivers or woods. It made the sighting of them all the more precious; a good omen.

And now the villagers of Bos'cairn Mor, splashing through puddles and thick mud to find a good viewing point, could hear them as they hummed a walking song. It was a happy song, full of optimism for the next home, the view that would be revealed over the next hilltop, although the strangely shaped bodies often fell out of tune with one another, or replaced the notes with clicks or chirrups, so as they got closer people grimaced at some of the grating sounds. The children laughed, thinking the clashing notes were funny, but danced to the tune nonetheless.

The Marvellous came to a field on the edge of the village, and instead of going around it, the troupe climbed, stepped or jumped over the hedge and walked straight across. Each footfall, each drop of spittle that flew from the mouths of the marchers as they hummed, was a shower of goodness on the ground. On the far side of the field, the farmer courteously opened the gate and nodded her thanks as the marchers passed. Outside, the road led directly to the centre of the village. The hum at a frantic pitch now, the March of the Marvellous continued.

They had finally become visible to the

villagers as they left the field. The high hedges, built as shelter from the wind, were enough to obscure all but the tallest Levanthian, but many of the Marvellous could look over them with ease. The first marcher through the gate had two long, thin arms that flapped in the breeze as if waving an over-excited greeting. The next, on all fours, leapt the gate, screeching in pleasure before returning to its high-pitched version of the hum. As they entered the village the marchers' discipline returned, and they made their way in single file. Bowls and barrels in every house had been filled with water and placed at the roadside, together with piles of fish, bread or any other food the villagers had available. The Marvellous, hungry and thirsty after days of non-stop travelling, were happy to accept. Hands of all shapes and sizes scooped water up to eager mouths, drinking a gallon or more at a time. One marcher, with a long, thick nose like a trunk, snorted and then sprayed water up and behind him, dousing the rest of the marchers. Sighs, squeals and brayed laughter interrupted the hum for a while as the water refreshed them. A small village girl, encouraged by her family, stepped forward and offered an apple. One of the taller marchers, her skull bisected narrowly and neatly down the centre, caught the girl's eye and stopped. She knelt down, getting as close to the girl's height as she could, and took the offering. A smile broke out on one side of her face and then appeared on the other. She broke the apple in two and placed a piece in each half of her mouth, then ruffled the girl's hair affectionately before getting back up and moving on.

Several of the villagers were attempting to count the marchers, but it was a confusing mass of bodies and, on later comparison, could not come up with a number they could agree on. But a happy morning was spent, watching the Marvellous pass through the village with such good grace and then disappear into the distance. Some said they could be seen, hours later, silhouetted against the skyline as they climbed a hill, still searching for their next home. For most, it was the first and only time they would see the March of the Marvellous. It was an extraordinary event in an extraordinary land.

Some appreciated the Marvellous in a different way. Their scarcity meant they were worth more than their weight in gold to those who placed a value on these things. One such Levanthian was Praze, who loved his country but found his countrymen naïve and backwards looking. He derided the world outside Levanthia but found their belief in wealth as the ultimate power far more worthy of respect than the reverence shown in magic by those around him. Magic was unreliable.

And, as the body in The Museum floating in formaldehyde could testify, it was certainly no match for a well-placed bullet.

The Museum was a private place, a secret place to most, and Praze remembered it now as he stood under the trees, watching the Marvellous as they set up their bivouac for the night. The Museum was in Australia, one of the Bloodstained Lands and not that great a distance from Levanthia itself, although its inhabitants, the Lesser Blood, were unaware of it. His client, Andrews, clearly thought of himself as an archivist of the mysterious. He had all kinds of artefacts relating to Lesser Blood legends, mostly for his own pleasure but also for certain individuals who would appreciate them, or who would barter the experience for something of acceptable worth. As far as Praze was aware, only one or two people had been allowed to view the example of the Marvellous, but they had been the right people—Andrews was now keen to get another, fresher specimen for a client of his own. Reluctant to give away too many details—in other words, aware that Praze would happily cut out the middleman and pocket double the fortune he had already been paid—Andrews had only let it be known that a group of pioneering scientists were keen to extract the DNA from one of the Marvellous, with a view to creating a hybrid. Lesser Blood with the power of the Marvellous? Praze snorted in his hiding place. It was impossible, but that was not going to be for him to worry about. It was perfectly possible though, he'd pointed out, to get a DNA sample from a living specimen—with or without their consent—but apparently that wouldn't be good enough in this case.

They need the cadaver for dissection, were Andrews' unspoken words.

It was all the same to Praze. Perhaps a living specimen would have presented some ethical problems—vivisection, after all, being such a primitive way of collecting information—but a corpse was a corpse, and much easier to transport.

What Praze was hoping for was that one of the adults would be restless during the night and separate from the group for a while. His rifle—a beautiful, antique hunting rifle from the Bloodstained Lands, modified by a Levanthian craftswoman to be almost silent—and his superb night vision would do the rest. The hardest part would be getting the body into the trees quickly and quietly, without waking anyone up. A group of the Marvellous would be difficult to escape; prison would be terrible for business.

In other countries, in other cultures, the Marvellous would be treated as shameful deformities, freaks of nature who would be better off dead. Or Changelings, swopped for healthy human babies by faerie folk during the night. No one knew why the Marvellous existed. Their births came entirely at random. For a Levanthian family it was seen as a blessing, tempered with the heartbreak of knowing their child would soon leave them to join their nomadic other family.

Elder had been dreaming of her birth family when she awoke. She'd seen them only once in the last sixty years, when the marchers had passed close to her hometown. Her parents had embraced her in sadness and pride, only reluctantly letting her go again. She wondered how her life would have been if she'd been born as Greater Blood. Given the choice, she would not swap her life, her body, for that of an ordinary Levanthian.

Elder was a pair of twins. Her cells had absorbed those of her sister when in the womb but instead of being destroyed, parts of the twin remained; the eye on the back of her balding head, the second pair of hands that grew out of her wrists. Elder only had partial control of these things. She could not direct where the eye looked, but she saw what it saw. She could not always direct her second pair of hands, but she felt what they touched. Each member of the Marvellous was unique, but what they had in common was the ability to *make change occur*—the practise of magic. In addition, their senses were heightened to a degree that was only possible in others— Greater and Lesser Blood alike—with the help of hallucinogens. With the assistance of her twin, Elder was even more aware of everything around her. She saw the world in 360 degrees, a massive spectrum of colour and ultraviolet vision. Able to see the stars by day as well as by night, she had a sure sense of where she was at all times. Not just in relation to Levanthia, but her place in the world and further, to the outer edge of the Solar System. She could feel the Earth's orbit around the Sun, the movement of the expanding Universe, and of the ripples in the air caused by the movement of an insect's wings.

She was not, however, aware of Praze hiding in the trees.

She overlooked his presence, so focused was she on Geddes, who had been gone from the camp for some time. Geddes was old and no longer agile; he might have fallen in the dark. She left the camp and relieved herself behind a rock, then had a look around. There was all kinds of movement in the air, the most deafening scents. Amongst it was a trace of Geddes, so she set off in search.

He appeared to be heading east, to the woods, a few hundred yards away.

She walked, as she usually did, in a state of euphoria, despite her concern. Surrounded by such a constant bombardment of the senses, she was aware of cutting her way through the air, of the creatures running from the vibrations made by her footsteps. Her third eye peered through the darkness behind her.

So it was with the greatest surprise that she came upon a shape rising in front of her, before turning to reveal Praze, with Geddes' limp body secured to a sled.

Praze, too, was shocked to come face to face with one of the Marvellous. Seeing the old man trying to manoeuvre in the dark was too good an opportunity to miss. A clean shot to his heart gave him a merciful, quick death. Praze did not think he'd been distracted by the task of strapping the body to the sled, although he was aware of a slight anxiety that hadn't been there the first time he had done this; Praze knew he was dealing with powerful forces and even his luck could only be pushed so far. He hurried to get the body onto the sled, only briefly pausing to check the man was dead. When the corpse was finally in place he turned, meaning to haul the sled to the safety of the woods, where he could load it onto his vehicle. Instead he was shocked to find that another of the Marvellous had crept right up to him without his knowledge.

He was grabbed by two pairs of hands. The woman hissed, spraying spittle over his face.

"What have you done?" she demanded.

Any hope Praze had of claiming that he was helping an injured marcher was lost; the woman could clearly see the rifle slung across his back. The best he could hope for now was that her feelings for her fellow were stronger than her anger.

"I think he's still alive," he said. "Just."

She relaxed her grip. Saving a life was more important than dragging him to the authorities. As Elder reached down with two left hands, Praze slipped out of her remaining grasp. He hesitated momentarily—his choice was to run, empty-handed, or battle for the body with someone clearly stronger than him. He chose to run and remain free. Elder's desire for Geddes to still be alive gave him enough time to sprint away and he was close to the woods when her screams of grief echoed around the land.

Praze needed to regroup. He was too far from home, his favoured retreat, but a business associate lived reasonably close by, so he made his way there. O'men owed him a favour or two; now was the time to call those favours in.

O'men was alone, as usual, and working, as usual, and not overjoyed to see Praze, but Praze's declaration that the slate could be wiped clean brightened his mood. Owing people—especially people like Praze—was always a last resort. Praze needed to rest and eat and used the time to tell O'men almost everything. Two heads would be better than one at solving his problem. And O'men was in no position to tell tales.

He was, however, well placed to be pious.

"You've killed one of the Marvellous? Are you insane? That's disgusting! I want you to leave."

"That isn't the problem. I had to leave the body and I need it for a client."

"The Marvellous are sacred," screeched

O'men. "And more powerful than a hundred of us. You hunted one down for a business transaction? Not for one of the Greater Blood, surely? I don't want you here—there's no hiding place from the Marvellous. The law will come down on you like a ton of bricks. I don't want to go to prison with you—forever. No one's done such a thing before!"

"Actually, there's no specific law against killing the Marvellous," said Praze.

"There doesn't need to be," flapped O'men. "It's obvious that it's the worst thing you could do."

Praze held up his hand for quiet. "It's no worse than some of the things you've done to the Lesser Blood over the years—and my client is one of them. I don't have time to pontificate over morals. That body's been paid for—I need to get it to its new owner and the sooner it's out of Levanthia, the better. Do the Marvellous cremate their dead? If so, how long have I got before they do it?"

O'men sat in silence. He was tempted to lie, to say the body would be ashes by now, but Praze wouldn't leave it at that. He'd be out hunting the Marvellous again.

"They bury their dead. Most likely where they died. If you're lucky the marchers would have done that and moved on by the time you get back there."

"Perhaps I should wait a while, make sure they've gone?" Praze mused.

O'men shook his head. "I've heard their bodies decompose very quickly. You don't have much time."

Praze shot O'men a suspicious glance. Was

the man just trying to get rid of him? There were all kinds of stories about the Marvellous. The truth was anyone's guess. Even so, better safe than sorry; hunting yet another member of the Marvellous was not an idea he relished.

O'men packed him some provisions and watched him leave, relief evident on his face. Praze could have told him that this was the last time he would ever approach the Marvellous and that if he was caught he wouldn't mention that O'men had harboured him—he did have some principles— but there was no harm in making the man sweat a little. It was a little power he could still wield over a weak and sentimental associate. He guessed O'men would immediately begin a cleansing ritual to wipe all trace of Praze's presence from his home. Magic had its place, Praze knew, but he refused to rely on it. The Greater Blood could be so *olde worlde* at times.

The Marvellous had gathered as soon as Elder had begun howling. It was always a big occasion when one of their number died, but in these unique circumstances—murder—the grieving took on a different hue. Geddes had been shot through the heart and would have died instantly; the killer had given Elder false hope that she could save Geddes, just so he could escape.

Powerful as the Marvellous were, Geddes' pulverised heart was irreparable and so there was no changing the situation. Elder was beside herself with grief and anger, some of which she directed at herself. She'd had the killer and had let him go. But why had he done it? It was an inexplicable act—for the Greater Blood, that was. Had one of the Lesser Blood found his way to Levanthia? Was such a thing possible? Either way, the whole of Levanthia would soon be searching for him. The killer would be found.

Geddes' funeral took place at first light. Songs were sung, thanks was given for the life Geddes had lived, the difference that had marked him out from the Greater Blood and thus made it necessary for him to join them. He was buried in a stone-lined grave, on his side, knees bent so he was almost in a foetal position. A massive, flat stone sealed the grave and stones and boulders were placed on top to form a monument. The Marvellous' powers were not used in the burial; grief was painful, living without loved ones required effort and focus and this was reflected in the work of the burial. The funeral, however, had contained magic in order to heighten the sense of celebration. The air had sparkled and strange birds had been created—a new species in Geddes' name, a dazzling delight of blue, orange and red, a hovering bird to sip nectar from the flowers.

When the monument was finished, the Marvellous packed up camp. Geddes would quickly return to the earth and there would be time to mourn as they marched. They set off as a group, although it was incomplete. Elder stayed.

Elder was waiting.

Praze was in a hurry, but he approached the area with caution, parking in a different part of the woods and circling around the back of what had been the camp. It was clear the Marvellous had moved on. Praze hoped that O'men was right and they hadn't cremated the body or taken it with them. He had no idea what he was looking for, but as soon as he saw the monument, he knew that he'd found the grave. It looked quite ordinary—just a pile of stones on the ground. No elaborate headstone, no magic occurring around it. He circled the monument, wondering if there was an entrance, cursing his luck when he found none.

He removed the first few stones then, realising how long it would take to clear the grave, sat and summoned all the power he had. He gave the stones a brief burst of life and an urge to disperse. Stones flew in all directions. Praze lay flat as they whizzed past his head. The ground rocked and he found the capstone partially removed, the grave beneath exposed.

Praze's lack of practise in magic, as well as his lack of subtlety, had tired him and he was relieved to see that there was room for him to remove Geddes' remains without shifting the heavy capstone any further. He crouched over the grave and peered in.

The smell of putrefaction nearly knocked him sideways. Was this an older grave? This couldn't be from a body dead less than twenty-four hours.

It could be if O'men had been right.

Praze took a gulp of fresh air and looked further into the grave. He was vaguely aware that he might be the first of the Greater Blood to have ever seen inside the grave of one of the Marvellous, but it was of no real interest to him. Through the darkness he could see the body was in an advanced state of decay. All that was visible was a disgusting mess of bones and mush running down between the stones. There was undoubtedly enough—if he scraped it up with his hands—to provide a DNA sample, but it wouldn't be enough—Andrews was expecting a cadaver. There was no way to confirm it, but this had to be the body of the man he'd killed; there were no other monuments in the area and it fitted with what O'men had told him. There was nothing for it but to track the Marvellous and kill another of their number. He sat back on his heels, exhausted at the thought.

And that was when Elder grabbed him.

O'men had wiped all trace of Praze's visit from his home. Forensically, even psychically, it was as if the man had never been there. But what Praze had confessed—casually, as if it were nothing more than a business issue to resolve—lay in his stomach like a stone.

Praze was behaving like Lesser Blood; like someone with no comprehension of the wider consequences of his actions. This could change the Marvellous' relationship with the Greater Blood, with Levanthia. This could change the Marvellous themselves.

But if the killer were apprehended, the body returned to its grave, it might be possible to limit the damage. Praze had described the Marvellous' camp well enough for O'men to have narrowed its location to two areas. If they were still there, he could warn them. If they—and Praze—had gone, he could track the man to whichever port he'd taken the remains to.

Turning Praze in would be his empowerment and penance all in one.

Elder could barely see Praze through the colours of her fury. While her instincts had told her the killer would return to claim Geddes' body—and had convinced the rest of the group to leave her behind temporarily—she had underestimated the weight of her grief and had slept through Praze's desecration. Thankfully he hadn't yet entered the grave or taken Geddes' bones.

She clasped the man to her; he would not slip away this time. She felt the blood pumping around his body, his heart rate increasing as he realised he was caught.

He was Greater Blood.

The shock of such a betrayal would have had her reeling if she hadn't been so intent on keeping hold of her prey. She turned him around and held his face close to hers. Every muscle on his ugly face twitched, his fresh sweat already rank.

"Why would you do such a thing? Do you even understand what you've done?" she bellowed.

"I was defending myself. He attacked me."

Nonsense spilled from Praze's mouth before he could stop it. It was obvious he was lying—the shot had been taken at long range and besides, if he'd been attacked then why would he return to rob the grave?

"You executed Geddes! We feel it when one of us dies. Geddes died because it was in your interests for him to do so. I can see the lies burrowing out of your skin. I want to know why."

Lying was pointless. And the truth would only make the woman even angrier, if that was possible, so Praze said nothing.

Elder pulled his jaw open and used her second hand to find his tongue. She pulled it out as far as it would go and then a little further. And a little further still.

"If you won't speak now, perhaps I should make sure you never do so again."

Praze's eyes indicated he was ready to talk, although when Elder let his tongue go he found it difficult to do anything other than groan in pain. As soon as he was able, he told her about Andrews and his demands for a specimen. He did his best to imply that Andrews was threatening him, but he knew he was embarrassingly transparent.

The air around Elder boiled with rage. Both were aware that she was close to killing him. In desperation, she threw Praze down into Geddes' grave and ordered the capstone back into place.

He wanted to scream but that would have made his situation worse; his only chance to stay sane was to find out if the woman was nearby and to negotiate his way out.

"I can give you Andrews!" he shouted, then vomited as the taste of decay turned his stomach.

Elder didn't want Andrews. The Lesser Blood's lack of morals were of no interest to her — but when they intruded into Levanthia and involved the collusion of Greater Blood, then something had to be done. But further desecration wasn't the answer. She would drag Praze out of the grave—as soon as her rage had subsided a little.

He could hear her nearby, sitting on the ground, muttering. Being left to suffocate with a corpse for company was probably the worst way he could think of to die. She hadn't left him. There was hope.

"Just take me to the authorities," he shouted. "I've done wrong. I'll go quietly."

Geddes' body was still decomposing around him and underneath him. There was very little room in the grave. Praze's face was pressed against the skull, able to see the last of its flesh dripping off its nose. Underneath him the freezing stones threatened to wrack him with cramp, but he dared not move the skeleton. His only chance was to show remorse. To transgress further was not an option.

He must have fainted. Suddenly awake, his first hope was that it was claustrophobia; the choking illusion that the confined space was moving, slowing closing in on him. Then he thought he heard a scraping sound, stone moving against stone. Was the frightful woman going to crush him to death? As quickly and carefully as he could, he reached out and touched the walls of the grave. They were still.

Praze stopped breathing for a few moments; he wanted to listen. Geddes' liquefying body dripped onto the stones and fizzed as it sought the spaces between them, where it could soak into the earth. The space around him was alive. He wondered what his own blood or flesh would do here—he was Greater Blood, of course, but it hadn't occurred to him before that what he was made up of might hold its own power. He was almost tempted to injure himself to find out, but movement caught his eye. Something was making its way through the darkness, between the stones, up into the grave.

It was a butterfly. Horribly crushed, presumably by the stones as they were laid. Its wings were torn and its body was almost flat. As it hauled itself out of the mush of Geddes' remains, the magic began. Praze watched as the insect was healed, as it moved from death to beautiful life, flapping its repaired wings to dry itself. Sad, then, that it would die here, thought Praze. He could hear it breathing, could see each breath merge with the appalling air of the grave. The butterfly began to flutter around. Optimistically, thought Praze. It actually expected to escape.

The capstone was pulled aside.

Praze had a fleeting glimpse of pleasure as the butterfly was released into the dazzling sunlight, emerging from its stone cocoon. He raised his head to take in the fresh air, the moment ruined as Elder dragged him out by his hair.

She sat on a boulder. "We've never been hunted before. Murdered to order. This is unprecedented and will be treated as such. You'll be in prison for the rest of your life. Or perhaps they'll exile you to the Bloodstained Lands. Since you love the Lesser Blood so much, perhaps you should live among them."

Now he was out of the disgusting hole in the ground, Praze began to tire of the sound of the woman's voice as it ranted on, the two sets of hands gesturing piously as the lecture continued. He knew something she didn't. For all the power and wisdom of the Marvellous, he knew something none of them did.

"The Marvellous have been here for thousands of years," he said. "One of you must have been murdered before. Even from a feud among yourselves. There must have been some suspicious deaths."

"There's been strange deaths, a disappearance, in my lifetime. Never murder."

"Maybe the man who disappeared got tired of your way of life. Maybe he went back to his birth family," said Praze, growing in confidence.

Elder stared coldly at him.

"Veil disappeared ten years ago. We felt he'd died but we couldn't tell how. Or where he was. We searched but never found him."

She stared at him a while longer. Both were silent. Then she got up.

"We'll go to the nearest town to hand you in." She grasped the back of his neck and forced him to his feet.

They would walk. The Marvellous always walked. It was around fifteen miles to the nearest town — enough time to make a plan. If he couldn't escape on the journey, he'd make a deal with the local police. It was possible to escape prison. He'd stake his reputation on it.

But first he had to survive the journey; he had two hands gripping his neck so tightly the vertebrae were separating. He shouted for her to stop, that she would break his neck if she continued. She walked on for a while, pushing him in front of her, before letting go. Praze had a moment of freedom, but before he could react he yelped in pain as Elder's hands crushed his shoulder instead.

"I don't mix with the Greater Blood," said Elder. "The Marvellous prefer the uninhabited places. But I know how we're regarded. What in the world could you have been offered to make hunting us acceptable?"

Praze kept his silence, knowing that no answer would be tolerable to her. Elder began another speech, about what a fool he was for believing he could get away with such a crime.

The pain in his shoulder was excruciating, the bones liable to shatter at any moment. Elder came to a sudden halt.

"How did you know our disappeared comrade was male?"

In raging agony, he lashed out with the one thing he'd wanted to keep from her.

"You Marvellous aren't that clever. Your comrade's a trophy now, in a rich man's house!"

And Elder released him.

June 21st, Winter Solstice in Levanthia, a time for change and renewal. O'men wondered what bearing it'd had on the events of the last few days. Praze's transgression was unimaginably huge. The threat of blackmail—of revealing O'men's less than pure character—was a weak one in comparison, and O'men had been even weaker to cave in.

He was certain there were only two areas of woodland surrounded by moor that could be the place where Praze had murdered one of the

Marvellous. He'd driven to the first, trekking around the place until he was satisfied Praze had not been there. He prayed he hadn't made a mistake and the second area was the correct one; if he was wrong, Levanthia might lose another of the Marvellous.

Praze looked at her deformed face and wondered why such people were so revered in his country, then crushed the thought in case Elder could read his mind. Although what did it matter now? He couldn't be in prison for any longer than for the rest of his life.

"You hunted Veil for sport? For money?" hissed Elder, her face so close to Praze's that he could see the splits in her tongue.

"Where is he?" she demanded.

"He's in the Bloodstained Lands. I did it for money. Not for fun."

Elder's anger was increasing. "Is his head hung on someone's wall? Is he dinner-time entertainment?"

Praze felt affronted. "It's far more dignified than that. My client's a serious collector. I shot Veil through the heart. Apart from that, he's intact. He stands in a tank of formaldehyde. My client has great respect for the Greater Blood. For the Marvellous."

"So much that he has to own one of us?"

They would all have to grieve again, now they knew what had befallen Veil. But all was not lost—if his body could be found, it could be returned to Levanthian soil. Some essence of Veil would remain. But the man who knelt before her felt not a scrap of remorse, was thinking of nothing more than talking his way out of the morass he'd got himself into.

"You have everything you could want in Levanthia," she said. "The land, the water, the air, is saturated with magic. So many things are possible in such a powerful place."

"I find money's more powerful than magic," replied Praze. "And even more is possible with it."

And that's when Elder lost patience with him.

O'men stood at the edge of the woods and gazed across the moor. It looked peaceful enough, although there was an air of something brutal having happened here. This was the place; he'd found bullet casings nearby and the rocky outcrop on the moor was just as Praze had described it. Further along was a cairn, a monument, to one of the Marvellous. He'd heard of them but had never seen one. Were the remains of the man Praze had killed buried there? O'men hoped so. The monument looked complete, so perhaps Praze hadn't been able to rob it. Though this might mean, of course, that he was hunting the Marvellous again.

He left the cover of the trees and crossed the moor. He reckoned on being able to find traces of the Marvellous—and Praze—near the cairn, and could track them from there.

He was nearly there when he noticed the birds. Corvids were everywhere—flocks of rooks, ravens, jackdaws and crows were wheeling and arguing. Something significant had certainly happened. When he saw what it was he nearly turned and fled, before gathering his courage and approaching.

It was Praze. He appeared to be levitating, a few feet above the heather, face up and spread-eagled.

And he was covered in birds.

O'men went closer, then ran up and scared the birds away before turning aside and vomiting.

It was Praze the birds were fighting over. The Marvellous had executed him, then, and performed a sky burial. He'd been draped over wooden stakes and disembowelled, an invitation to the birds and other creatures to feed on him until only the bones remained.

The birds returned almost immediately; there was too much good food available not to. A closer glance—O'men couldn't bear more than that—revealed flies and other insects gorging on what remained of his intestines. Praze had been an arrogant man, incapable of respect. Shocking as his fate was, O'men was not surprised that his deeds had finally caught up with him. At least now he was finally giving something back to Levanthia.

Praze's eyes had been left open, staring skyward. The man didn't deserve it, but O'men thought he should look as if he was at peace. He raised his hand to close the lids.

And the eyes, sensing movement, flickered. It was only then that O'men realised just how severe the Marvellous' punishment had been.

Praze was a living sky burial.

O'men screamed for hours but the sound did not scare the birds away from their feast.

The Hidden

'Welcome to the Chapel Estate'.

The board at the estate's entrance, tagged with hieroglyphic graffiti, displayed a map that gave no hint of the house she was looking for. It had been a long walk from Pengethon station through a town with more shops empty than trading, drugs furtively dealt in the market square and people shuffling around the streets, aware their hometown had seen better days.

This was not the Cornwall of her holidays.

The naïveté of the thought embarrassed her. As a child she had travelled through this place on the train, heading towards the golden sands and rocky coves of the west. How could she not have seen it? The great Carn Brea hill loomed overhead, its long spine marked at one end with a castle, at the other a pyramid shaped monument. She remembered seeing the hill, but not the town that sat at its foot. Nearby a donkey brayed; a jeering tone. She entered the estate and began walking—she would ask one of the residents for directions if necessary. After all, there were not likely to be any other guest houses in the area.

The guest house's website, which she'd only found by chance, had not claimed great things of

The Winter House, but it did promise clean, comfortable rooms at a bargain price. The website was amateurishly put together and didn't even contain any photographs, but the chance to escape the city for a while was too good to miss. She'd be a short bus ride from the sea; a few days spent walking on deserted beaches with the luxury of someone else cooking breakfast sounded heavenly.

It was an old Council estate, the houses now privately owned. The pride of ownership showed in little touches on the houses, sparks of individuality in the front gardens. She took a path beside an empty children's playground, towards a signpost that stood at a junction near the playground entrance. It only added to her confusion. She stopped at the crossroads and wondered which way to go. The wooden signpost, its lower half covered in glistening moss, pointed confidently down the narrow estate roads. Rebecca took out her O.S. map, without any expectation of finding the places marked on the signpost, and was not disappointed. 'Ignis', 'Aer', 'Aqua', 'Terra'; could they possibly be areas of the estate or even tiny hamlets outside it, too insignificant to be marked? They were such strange names, even for Cornwall, which was full of unpronounceable villages.

She had to pick a route. Looking along each of the roads, she found one of them gently made its way uphill and around a corner. It felt like the right direction. So she made her way towards Aer.

The road turned and ran parallel to Carn Brea, the houses having uninterrupted views of the hill. It would be the perfect place for a guest house. Rebecca picked up her pace, hoping she had not already passed it.

As it happened, The Winter House was impossible to miss.

It stood, three houses converted into one, in its substantial garden, with a granite wall surrounding it. Its name was inscribed on the gate but was, in the circumstances, absurdly unnecessary.

On this mid-May day The Winter House—and its gardens—were covered in snow.

Rebecca looked up and down the road, needing someone to confirm what she was seeing. A woman and her child were approaching. They passed The Winter House without more than a longing look from the child. Incredulous, Rebecca stopped them.

"Oh yes, that's The Winter House," said the woman, in answer to Rebecca's enquiry. "I've never stayed there of course but I hear it's very comfortable."

"Is the snow a gimmick? It looks real."

"Of course it's real. It's always been like that. I usually have to drag this one past—he'd play in the garden all day." The woman pressed on. There was nothing to do but go in. After all, she'd booked and paid for a room.

She walked up to the gate. The snow stopped on the outer edge of the wall. She laid her hand along the top of the stone. The snow was real enough; its coldness was shocking. She pulled her jacket sleeve over her hand, opened the gate and went through. Stopping several times to crouch and scoop up snow, or to brush it off the branches of a bush, it took some time to reach the front door.

There were tracks in the snow, footsteps leading from the door around the side of the house. Rebecca exhaled and watched as a puff of air appeared. It was a beautiful, snowy winter scene. And so ordinary that she had to look back towards the road to remind herself which season it really was.

She realised she was shivering with cold and zipped her jacket up to the neck, then reached up and knocked on the door.

Robert Goodfortune put on his coat and left his room. The wind rushed around, as it always did, touching each corner of The Winter House, before settling into the cracks. He walked down the stairs and was heading for the front door when he heard voices coming from the lounge. He looked in to see a woman talking to Patrick Chalice, the elderly owner. A new guest! This was not an everyday occurrence. Robert glanced at his face in the hall mirror, knowing that it was likely to stop her in her tracks. Most of the locals now ignored how he looked but some, especially outsiders, were frightened or angered by him.

As a child, Robert Goodfortune had met with an accident.

He had been watching a bird, the tiniest and most beautiful he had ever seen. No bigger than a ladybird, it had settled on the petal of a flower. As he bent over it, it had opened its wings and, in a burst of amazing colour flown up and hit him in the face.

Or so he had thought at first. In fact, the bird had passed through the centre of his left eye. From that day on it had fluttered constantly around inside his head. Over the years he had learned to live with it, although there were still times when he found it disorientating.

The bird had left its mark on his face. The white of his eye was splattered with colours, his eyelid and the area around it patterned in purple, turquoise and green, like an unusual tattoo or a bizarre birthmark. His mother had said he was blessed. Others were not so kind. He had been attacked by people who saw his difference as a threat. He hoped this woman did not see him as such. They were, after all, to be neighbours.

As she strode towards him, he offered to carry her bag upstairs, much to Chalice's relief.

"There's no need, thanks," said Rebecca, her rucksack firmly in her grip. "But you can walk up with me. Tell me a bit about this place."

Rebecca looked him full in the face, noting his appearance but not commenting. What she really wanted was a hot bath and a drink, but a few minutes' conversation about the house might answer a lot of questions. The old man had given her nothing except a promise that her room would be warm.

Her room was by the top of the stairs, at the opposite end of the floor to Robert's. She'd asked him how long he'd been staying and he answered, "For too long, I imagine. I'm never quite where I ought to be." Then she asked what she really wanted to know—why The Winter House was covered in snow on a spring day, to which he replied, "This house is in a permanent state of winter."

He didn't elaborate and she was tired, so

she let him go on his way. Alone, she looked around the room. It was designed for functionality rather than character; its social housing roots more obvious here than on the outside, which was camouflaged by snow. But it was homely enough, with an open fire roaring away next to the bathroom. The décor was a bit eccentric—an old, torn section of wallpaper positioned near the bed looked as if it had been forgotten about when the room was last redecorated. Its scruffiness was out of keeping.

She took out her phone. She always rang or texted her parents whenever she was away, but there was no signal. The old man would know of a phone box nearby. She ran a bath. As she lay in the wonderful, hot water, she thought about Patrick Chalice. He'd been pleased to have another guest and had wanted to know how her journey had been. When she'd mentioned that she'd come via the crossroads, he'd smiled.

"The Crossroads of the Four Elements!" he exclaimed. "It's not easy to find. I've never seen it myself."

"I'm not surprised," she replied. "None of the places that it points to are marked on my map. There was no sign for the guest house, either. It was only by luck that I chose this way."

"Well, you made the right choice. The village of Aqua," (he pointed in one direction), "lies under a lake, Ignis," (he pointed upwards), "is on the surface of the Sun and Terra," (a final, dramatic gesture), "is underground. Here is definitely the best place."

He was talking to her as if she was a child. Not wanting to invite another whimsical answer, she didn't bother to ask about the snow. But Chalice was ordinary, even banal; undisturbed by the snow that covered his house, he simply kept the fire well stoked and wore a heavy jumper. To be so ordinary in such a situation was, in itself, extraordinary.

Rebecca closed her eyes and laid a little lower in the bath. The wind rattled around the windows of her room and, not finding a way in, made do with the outside.

"We have always been here."

Startled by the voice, she opened her eyes. The bathroom was empty, her room quiet. She'd been dreaming. She got out of the bath and dried herself in front of the fire. It was still well alight.

The phone box that Chalice had directed her to was working, much to Rebecca's relief. She rang her parents, not lingering on the details of her surroundings, only describing Pengethon as 'a slightly sad place' where she was unlikely to spend much time.

Now she was back in the spring evening, a drink was called for. She returned to the pub she'd passed at the edge of the estate, bought a beer and headed for the garden, which sat next to a stream. There she found the young man with the marks on his face. He was sitting alone, his drink untouched on the table while he stared at the water.

"Do you mind if I join you for a minute?" she asked.

He seemed surprised but nodded and sat quietly, expecting her to speak. Rebecca thought it would have been obvious that she wanted to talk about the guest house, but it clearly wasn't the case.

"Why is it covered in snow? You said it was always winter there. What does that mean?"

"It always has been," he replied. "As far back as when The Winter House opened, anyway. It obviously suits the building to be this way."

"Doesn't anyone find it strange? How is it possible?"

He frowned as if he didn't quite understand the question. "It's not strange for The Winter House. There are lots of places which are constantly in other states of being. It depends on who had the houses converted, and why, I suppose. I assume it was their intention."

Rebecca sighed. The young man seemed intelligent enough but wasn't helping. He noticed her frustration.

"It's different here," he said. "Take that stream. It's in full flow. Have a look at it."

She could see straight away that the stream was dry. She walked right to its edge and crouched down, looking closer.

There were fish in it; swimming as if the stream was, in fact, in full flow. She reached down to touch the bed of the stream and put her hand into *something*. A fish swam between her open fingers.

"It feels like... air," she said.

"That's exactly what it is. You could say it's water with a chemical imbalance."

Her hand felt odd. She moved it around then withdrew it. It was dry but cold.

"You know, I came through here a dozen times as a child. I saw the hill but I never knew this place existed. I'm sure the train stopped at Pengethon but I never noticed it."

Robert smiled. "No one ever does. Places like this are invisible. Not through magic—people just choose not to see them."

"And is there anything else I should know about The Winter House?" asked Rebecca as she returned to her drink.

Robert Goodfortune thought for a while.

"Only that Room 3 doesn't exist. Your end of the floor has rooms 1 and 2, my end has rooms 4, 5 and my room, 6."

"Let me guess—whoever had the houses converted didn't like the number 3."

"Perhaps it was unlucky for them. I've never thought to ask. The Housekeeper will be making breakfast in the morning. You can ask her."

The Housekeeper, it seemed, had no other name. Rebecca had entered the house in a hurry, ducking out of a rain shower that had turned to snow as soon as she was through the gate. Chalice was stabbing at the fire in the lounge with a poker and reminded her when breakfast was served. Rebecca had nodded, unimpressed that Chalice referred to his staff by their position rather than by name. At breakfast the next morning, after a night of unsettling dreams, her attempts at friendly conversation were met with polite disinterest, although the Housekeeper had a little to say on the snow bound House.

"My family's lived in this town for longer than the estate's been here and the houses were ordinary when they were first built. Something must have happened during the conversion. The original owner lived in the middle of the three houses and was able to buy all of them. When he passed away, Mr Chalice took it on. He'd always wanted to run a guest house."

"Is there a reason why there's no room 3?"

The Housekeeper looked up sharply. "Some things just *are*."

Rebecca walked around the garden after she'd eaten. She took some photographs but couldn't capture the full oddness of the place. The bare bones of the winter trees just a few yards from the life of the outside world were difficult to portray; somehow they just didn't come out well. She'd read that some things weren't meant to be photographed—if that were true then this was one of them. She touched the trunk of a twisted hawthorn tree, preferring it in its bareness. It was like something from folklore; a person cursed for doing something forbidden. She picked up some snow, pressed it into a ball and threw it over the garden wall. It melted, as she knew it would, as soon as it crossed the boundary, water splashing down onto the grass outside. A few days here was not going to be enough.

Chalice was delighted that Rebecca wanted to stay on. Business was evidently poor.

"That's lovely, my dear. I'll let the Housekeeper know. Perhaps you've got your eye on Mr Goodfortune?"

Rebecca smiled through gritted teeth. "I want to explore a bit more. And since I may never find my way here again, I thought I'd better make the most of it."

She went to the far end of the house and

knocked at Room 6. Robert was in and seemed happy that she was staying on. She told him how the Housekeeper had reacted to her question about Room 3.

"This part of the estate is made up of three-bedroomed houses," she said. "Even allowing for en-suites, there's plenty of space for six rooms. And if there weren't, why leave out number three? If this was an older house I'd guess there was a hidden room. I bet the Council still have the plans for the conversion. I'd love to see them."

"The House is really bothering you, isn't it?" said Robert.

"This *estate* is really bothering me," Rebecca replied. Then something occurred to her. "What do you know of the Crossroads of the Four Elements? It's the weirdest signpost I've ever seen."

"I've walked all the paths the signpost points to. They are other stories for other days. But The Crossroads of the Four Elements is on the border between the *Known* and the *Not Known*. Cornwall is sometimes very far away from it; you could easily have ended up *Elsewhere* instead of here," said Robert.

"And what bothers me most of all is that no one's capable of a simple answer," said Rebecca. His fey, unconcerned manner was annoying. She walked out. Robert let her go, then thought better of it and went after her. But he didn't get very far.

Her end of the house now had three rooms.

Rebecca tramped through the snow and saw the Housekeeper sweeping one of the paths clear. The woman didn't look up from her work. Feeling the cold, Rebecca decided to put on some more suitable clothing and spend some time in the garden. Perhaps the reason for the snow was geological and could be explained scientifically. She would do some digging around, get some rock and soil samples, something tangible to leave with. She went back inside to find Robert Goodfortune staring at Room 3.

"Oh my God! What's inside?" she asked.

"I haven't been in. I've just been watching in case anything comes out."

Rebecca went to the door.

"I wouldn't recommend going in," Robert continued. "A room that can suddenly appear can also suddenly disappear, I should think."

"Aren't you curious as to what's in there?"

"I'm more interested in *why*."

"Well, if someone's playing tricks, I want to know."

Rebecca reached for the door handle. It felt elusive, as if it wasn't quite *there*. Eventually she managed to get hold of it.

The door opened to reveal a solid wall.

Rebecca laughed. "Is that it? It's like a bad haunted house at a funfair."

Robert approached the open door, hesitated, then walked into the wall. It dissolved around him.

"A simple façade," he said, although Rebecca was beyond hearing; for inside the room were the other three seasons of the year.

Spring, summer, autumn; all vied for space within Room 3. Hot sunshine competed with blustery showers and swirling fog. The smell of summer rain washed away the scent of spring flowers then the autumn wind blew the rain away as quickly as it appeared. It was chaos. She ran back to her room. Robert reluctantly left, closing the door carefully behind him, and went to her. She tried to speak without screeching.

"I heard voices last night. I never remember my dreams but I had a nightmare about little men walking on their hands and now this! Tell me why I shouldn't leave?"

Robert's eyes widened at the mention of her dream. "Were their heads on back to front so they could see where they were going?"

She thought for a while. "I think so. What I remember most was a horrible, smoky atmosphere."

"Perhaps you should leave," he said.

She looked insulted. "Are *you* leaving?"

He shook his head.

"Well, I won't, either. I want to understand what's going on here."

So she stayed. Room 3 had disappeared again and so the days passed with nothing untoward happening, apart from the constant presence of the snow. Rebecca collected samples of soil, kicked up from the frozen ground by her boots, and some stones from the garden, along with one worked loose from the wall. What she'd do with them when she returned to London she didn't know, but she was sure it would be important, one day, to have evidence of this place.

Meanwhile, she investigated her room. There was nothing remarkable about it, apart from the scruffy section of wallpaper near her bed. Part of it had been torn away, presumably in the process of re-decorating. The decorator seemed to have given up at this point and hadn't even attempted to cover the old wallpaper up. Still, it meant the intriguing design was clearly visible. The shapes on it reminded Rebecca of the German woodcuts her father was so fond of. She wanted to ask Chalice or the Housekeeper about it but was aware that it would just sound like a petty complaint, an excuse to demand a discount. Rebecca lay in bed one evening and stared at the patterns. As she gazed, they began to form a picture; a forest set alight, figures running from it or consumed by the flames...

She shook her head and was back in the present. The wallpaper was just wallpaper. But she must have slept, because the moon was up, shining down onto the snow and lighting up the slopes of Carn Brea. She was suddenly aware of the smell of summer rain, the downpour after a hot spell her favourite part of a season that was hard to endure in London. Had the third room reappeared? She opened her door and crept along the corridor.

Room 3 had indeed re-materialized. It stood where the wall had been. She had run her hand along the corridor there the previous day, expecting trickery, but had found nothing. Now sunlight peeked under the door and from the keyhole.

Robert's room was too far away; Room 3 might disappear before she could go and get him. It was a chance to gather her courage and see what was really in there.

The door opened—with difficulty, as before—to reveal the wall, but this time it was less convincing; the smell of the seasons inside was drifting through.

She brushed the wall aside. The room was full to bursting point, barely containing its reluctant guests. She wanted to go in but hesitated, afraid. Then the door was yanked from her grasp and slammed shut.

She expected to see the Housekeeper, but instead was faced with something that was the size of a toddler but had the face of a devil.

"Keep them in!" it shrieked. "We flourish in winter!"

As it spoke, more of the creatures pulled free of the skirting boards. One of them stood on its hands, its head swivelling 180 degrees to face her.

She had dreamt of these monsters.

The first one spoke again.

"You! Are from the world of the commonplace. Leave this door and this room alone. They no longer belong to you."

Rebecca backed away from them and, when they made no move to follow, began to run.

"They're Woodmen," said Robert. "My mother read me scary stories about them when I was young. I recognised them from your dream the other night. I wasn't sure if they were real. That's why I wanted you to go home. If you're dreaming of them, you might not be safe here."

"What are they? I've never heard of them."

"The stories said they were quite common centuries ago but were believed to be evil. People were afraid of them. Many were hunted down and burned alive. Some managed to escape and hid in trees—inside them, *becoming* wood. Hence the name. They've been found in the pages of books, disguised as drawings. They can be inside anything made of wood."

"Like wallpaper?" asked Rebecca, thinking of the section near her bed.

Robert covered his eyes for a moment. The bird was fluttering around inside his head. The feeling left him and he looked out of the window at the snow.

"The Woodman told you they prefer winter," he said. "So they've been living here and have put the rest of the seasons into a room that they've managed to hide most of the time. If we could let the seasons out, the Woodmen might die, or at least leave."

Rebecca wanted to laugh. The situation was ridiculous. She was still at home in London, dreaming. Nevertheless, killing the Woodmen—even in theory—was disturbing and she said as much to Robert.

"The Woodmen in the stories," he said, "are parasites. If they form an attachment to you, they burrow into you while you're asleep and leave a trace of themselves there. People *change*—ferns grow out of their skin, bushes climb up their throats and out of their mouths. They don't die from it—they can't. They become a living forest, a new home for the Woodmen."

Rebecca shook her head. This was not a dream; it was a dark, dark fairy tale. She remembered the Housekeeper's expression when she'd asked her about Room 3.

"I wonder if the Housekeeper knows something about this," she murmured.

"It'll be light in a few hours," said Robert.

"Get some sleep if you can and then we'll see what we can find out."

They did not share a table at breakfast; the Housekeeper would never help them if she felt they were ganging up on her.

Robert was on his third mug of tea before Rebecca could think of a way to start the conversation. As the Housekeeper brought her breakfast in, Rebecca smiled. The Housekeeper gave a slight nod in return.

"This place looks beautiful in the snow," Rebecca said. "But doesn't it get you down that it's like it all the time?"

The Housekeeper took a breath. "I'm used to it, dear. The air's always lovely and clear. Wouldn't have it any other way. Mr Chalice is happy here, too."

"And *they* prefer it this way," said Rebecca.

The Housekeeper stiffened.

"Did the owner bring them here when he had the houses converted?"

Robert took the cue and snorted.

"No one invites Woodmen into their home! My guess is that they were hidden in something used in the conversion. They could've been in any of the timber used. Maybe even the wallpaper." He winked his afflicted eye at Rebecca.

"It's nobody's fault," said the Housekeeper. "Mr Chalice is not even aware of them. Or of Room 3 coming and going. It bothered him terribly when it disappeared. But you get used to these things."

"Have you seen the Woodmen?" asked Rebecca.

"Once," said the Housekeeper. "I saw a

glimpse of something once. I wouldn't like to say what it was. I'd never sleep here."

She turned to go. Robert asked her one more question.

"Would you like them to leave?"

She shook her head. "Best keep things as they are. If they go from here, they'll find somewhere else and who knows what will happen then. If you're unhappy then you'd best check out."

Robert wished they'd never approached her. He'd been staying at The Winter House for months. Despite its mundane appearance, the estate was an remarkable place. He did not want to go elsewhere, although now he knew there were Woodmen in the house, he nervously wondered if he'd ever sleep soundly again.

He looked at Rebecca. She shrugged. It was unhelpful.

The catastrophe began to unfold after breakfast, although it could be argued that it had begun, like tipping the first domino in a line, when Rebecca had arrived in the estate.

Rebecca found the Housekeeper puzzling. She'd seemed almost protective of the Woodmen. But even Robert—strange Robert, afflicted by God knew what—was reluctant to actually do anything other than talk. Rebecca, however, was amazed by everything she'd seen on the estate. She needed to put it into context, to tell someone from the outside world who would see the situation for the miracle it was. When she got home she'd send her photos and samples to a science magazine but for now a call to a newspaper—a serious one—about a permanently snow-bound house, was required.

They would listen. She needed them to be amazed.

She rang the newsdesk of The Guardian from the phone box.

"I have a big story for you," she said to the woman who answered. "I've been staying at a guest house in Pengethon... "

"Where?"

"Pengethon. In Cornwall."

"Which coast is it on?"

"It's not on the coast, it's an old tin mining area. It doesn't matter—what matters is that this house is covered in snow. Has been for years, all year round. If it rains in the street, it snows on this house. Nothing else is affected. It's the most incredible thing I've ever seen."

Almost.

"Can you email me some photos? With today's paper in the picture?" There was no excitement in the reporter's voice.

"I can when I get back to London, but there's no internet signal here. You really need to see this for yourself. This is the biggest story you'll ever get."

Rebecca instantly regretted the cliché. The woman was almost laughing.

"Look," she said, "Email me the photos with proof of the date. And send me a link to a map so I know where it is. If it's anywhere near Padstow you might be in luck—the editor's there on holiday soon. He might drop by."

Rebecca knew she was wasting her time. The Winter House was a marvel, an impossibility. But it was on an estate in a deprived, unglamorous town. How could anything amazing be happening in such a place?

Rebecca walked back through the estate, her anger and embarrassment growing. She felt ridiculous. She knew that what she'd said had sounded like nonsense. The press would never be interested. It was not enough to send an email on her return home, politely asking to be taken seriously, politely pointing out one of the wonders of the world.

She walked through the garden of The Winter House, shivering, as she always did, at the sudden cold. She kicked at the snow and her boot met resistance. A rock. She brushed it clean and hid it in her jacket.

The rock would prop a door securely open. The next time Room 3 appeared would provide all the proof she needed.

And so the catastrophe came closer.

Robert was up by the monument on Carn Brea. He had spent many hours at the Neolithic settlement on the hill, sitting and focussing on the tiny bird inside his skull. One day, he hoped, it would find its way out again; he would feel something in his left eye and there it would be; free. If it should happen he wondered if his face would return to normal. The ability to be anonymous again would be liberating. But the little bird had changed the way he saw the world. He was more receptive to things since the accident, more aware of the peculiarity of life. He had seen much during his life and had come to Pengethon after hearing a rumour that something exceptional was there. And it was—The Winter House, and the estate around it, were a delight. He noted the stream, with its air-water, he found The Crossroads of the Four Elements—and the curious places it signposted—and had sat among the remains of the ancient settlements on the hill. Most importantly, he had realised that all these things were connected to one another. As were all things in all Universes. Even the Woodmen, he supposed. He wondered if he'd judged them harshly, believing in stories instead of finding the truth of the matter for himself. He needed to talk to them. Once again he blessed the little bird for what it had given him.

He stood by the monument and watched Rebecca Shadow heading purposefully towards The Winter House.

There was going to be trouble.

He began to make his way down.

The Housekeeper was in the garden, clipping back the bushes, when Rebecca arrived. The square, characterless house provided a strange backdrop to the Housekeeper, secateurs in hand, trug settled on the snow, every inch a country gardener. She cared about the place, that much was obvious. Perhaps to her the Woodmen were just part of the fixtures and fittings. Every house had its quirks.

Rebecca smiled at her and the Housekeeper nodded as usual.

"I've re-stocked the firewood in your room," said the Housekeeper. "It's going to snow again tonight, I think, so I wanted to make sure everyone would be warm."

It was as if their earlier conversation had

never taken place.

"Thanks," said Rebecca. "Is Patrick Chalice around?"

"He's gone to visit his sister. He'll be back later. Is there anything I can do?"

Rebecca shook her head, glad that he was out of the way, and went indoors.

The tea tray had been refilled so Rebecca made a drink. She lit the fire, not so much for the warmth as for the comfort of it. She looked out of the window and saw rain sweeping towards Carn Brea from the north. It would, of course, fall on The Winter House as snow.

The crackling of the kindling was soothing and she lay on her bed and dozed for a few minutes.

And then was wide awake.

Snow quietly gathered along the window-sill.

And she knew that Room 3 had reappeared.

What made the room come and go? Rebecca imagined that her need to see it was at least partly responsible this time. She sensed that something was different. The air was full of agitation, perhaps from the Woodmen, that the room was not entirely under their control. She grabbed her camera and the rock.

The door's handle, as usual, slipped in and out of solidity but at last she got a grip on it, opened it and wedged it open with the rock. She assumed the room couldn't disappear unless the door was closed, so it was safe to enter. She swept the pretence of the wall aside and went in.

The three seasons, confined in such a small

space, buffeted her. She was sprayed with rain, then hot sunshine beat down, glancing off the window and dazzling her. The sun disappeared behind a cloud and she could see again.

A Woodman had appeared. Another squeezed reluctantly from the door frame and dropped to the floor. It scowled at her, although the other Woodman appeared to be grinning.

"These seasons are the death of us!" exclaimed the scowling Woodman. "Close the door!"

"I will. Very soon." Rebecca kept her voice calm and her hands reasonably steady as she photographed the chaos inside the room. As far as she could see, the room itself looked like the others, although it was suffering from the constant effects of the weather—the carpet stank of damp and was rotting away from years of rainfall, the once-colourful bedding was faded by the sun.

A Woodman grabbed her leg.

"I'm leaving!" screamed Rebecca. Too late—the creature tore through her jeans and ran razor sharp claws down her calf.

She lost her grip on the camera, shook the Woodman off and ran for the open door. The wind began to whip up and rain suddenly lashed across the room. Robert and the Housekeeper appeared as she stepped back into the corridor. The Housekeeper turned pale; she had not seen Room 3 since it had first disappeared and had only had the briefest sight of a Woodman.

The situation needed calming down. Robert ran his hands over his cropped hair and spoke to the nearest Woodman.

"Why are you in this house? Why did you choose this place?"

"We have always been here. This land's full of strange attraction. We lived in the gorse on the hillside, then made our way into the wood in this house. We know that we are safer in winter—they don't come hunting us then. We learnt how to keep this small area in that season. We're close to banishing the other seasons from here forever. She must stop."

Robert saw the rock propping open the door.

"What are you doing?" he asked.

"I've taken photos. Proof. This is too amazing to keep secret," said Rebecca, suddenly aware of the blood running down her leg.

"Well, I think we should leave them be," he said. "I didn't even know the Woodmen were here until you turned up."

"You said they were evil. Parasites. God knows what they might have done to you."

"But they haven't, have they? In all this time, I've never seen them. I've been thinking about the stories I read—to be turned into part of a forest might actually be wonderful. It doesn't mean the Woodmen are evil. People make things up to explain what they don't understand, to justify hating it. I know all about that."

The Housekeeper made for Rebecca. When they were face to face she spoke in a low, angry tone.

"And what about *him*?" she nodded towards Robert. "And the stream? And all the other miracles here? This is a very special place. That's why the Woodmen are here. What will happen to it all when the outside world knows about it?"

Rebecca hadn't thought about Robert. Or the affect on the rest of the estate if The Winter House became public knowledge. Rebecca wondered if she was acting out of a sense of wonder or hurt pride.

"But what about the snow?" she asked the Housekeeper. "What if we can release the other seasons from the room? Patrick Chalice must miss them. It can't be healthy to live like this."

"It is as it is," said the Housekeeper. "It's been this way since the houses were converted. Mr Chalice doesn't know any other way. Neither do the Woodmen. Everyone's safer like this."

Robert held his hands up for silence. The two women looked at him and, just for a second, saw a tiny bird fly across his left eye.

"We need to talk about this calmly," he said. "I'll get your camera, Rebecca, but I want you to delete the photos."

He pulled his collar up against the rainstorm that had begun again in Room 3 and went in. Rebecca's camera was lying in a puddle. Robert gently shook off the water, checked the camera was still working and put it in his pocket.

Rebecca watched him. She was relieved to see that he wasn't deleting the photos; he probably wanted to make a point to the Woodmen that she'd do it herself.

Then came the unmistakeable sound of stone scraping against wood. One of the Woodmen had picked up the doorstop. He hurled it in Rebecca's direction. She jumped back and heard it thud as it hit the Housekeeper. She fell to the floor and as Rebecca went to her aid the door to Room 3 swung shut.

And then it disappeared, leaving nothing but the corridor wall.

Robert was still inside.

Rebecca screamed. *Robert was still inside.*

Rebecca spent the next two days and nights alone in The Winter House. Patrick Chalice was there but his presence was ethereal. He was quite lost without the Housekeeper and Rebecca got her own supplies for her room while suffering his version of breakfast. She made excuses for the non-appearance of Robert Goodfellow, but all the while she was sick with worry, spending hours pacing the corridor or just staring at the wall, trying to will Room 3 into existence. Where had it gone? Was the room different when it wasn't in the guest house? Was Robert dead or alive? She went to the odd section of wallpaper in her room and implored the Woodmen to appear and help him.

There was no response. They did not emerge, either to gloat or to help. Had they achieved their ultimate aim—were the room and its seasons gone forever?

The nights were a trial. Rebecca didn't know which was worse—the hours of sleeplessness or waking suddenly to the eerie sound of tapping at the window to find hailstones blowing heavily against the building.

At last the Housekeeper reappeared. She had suffered a mild concussion and had been told to rest, but was anxious to get back to work. After a long discussion with Chalice, the Housekeeper sought Rebecca out, who nearly cried with relief when she saw her.

"Thank God you're okay."

The Housekeeper did not return Rebecca's smile and remained outside the threshold of the room. She kept glancing around, wondering where the Woodmen were. She asked where Robert was and was distressed when Rebecca told her he was still in Room 3.

"When will the room reappear?"

"I don't know. I've hardly moved from here, waiting for it. There doesn't seem to be a pattern."

"Are you happy for having caused so much trouble?" asked the Housekeeper. "We lived alongside the snow and ice and Room 3. Mr Goodfortune's been here for months with nothing terrible happening. God only knows what has happened to him or what will happen next."

There was a noise along the corridor. Both women started, hoping it was the reappearance of the room, Robert returned to them safe and sound, but the corridor remained as it was.

This time it would take more than wishing to see Room 3 again.

Rebecca returned her attention to the Housekeeper. "This is not my fault. Anyone would have done the same. I had the door propped open—it was the Woodman who moved the doorstop."

"You were the catalyst," said the Housekeeper. "You treated this guest house and one of its guests like a curiosity. Mr Chalice would like you to leave and I can't say I blame him."

Rebecca gaped at the Housekeeper. "I can't go. I can't leave Robert... wherever he is."

"Do you think Room 3 will return just because you're here? Now leave, and forget all about this place. Poor Mr Goodfortune must be suffering terribly."

Enough. Rebecca had been close to tears before the Housekeeper had begun berating her. She knew she had to shoulder some responsibility for what had happened, but leaving—running away—was surely the worst thing she could do. She was about to concede that contacting the press had been unwise when more noises came from the corridor, followed by a flash of intense, white light and the rumble of thunder.

Both women rushed towards it. Room 3 was not there. But the carpet was wet and lightning flickered from a crack in the skirting board. The air was heavy with a storm.

Still Room 3 did not appear.

"This is wrong," said Rebecca. "The seasons were locked in the room. Whenever I saw Room 3 they were completely confined inside it. Nothing like this happened."

She cautiously rested her hand against the wall. It was solid. There was no sense of anything laying beyond. There was another rumble of thunder which shook the building.

"Do you think it's Robert? Is he trying to get out?" Rebecca asked, more out of wishful thinking than belief. It was too chaotic to be anything good—more likely the Woodmen were finalising their plan to keep the seasons at bay.

The Housekeeper, holding back her fury as best she could, was about to order Rebecca to leave again but was silenced by the sight of Patrick Chalice, who had made his way up the stairs.

"Miss Shadow, the Housekeeper has made my wishes clear," he said. "Please vacate your room as soon as possible."

It was a plea rather than a demand.

"For your information," he continued, "I have been aware of all the things that go on in this house. I leave them alone and until now they've done the same for me."

Rebecca appealed to the man for mercy. "How can I leave with Robert still missing? Please—I want to help find him."

He shook his head. "It takes a particular kind of person to find the Crossroads of the Four Elements and so I thought it was good that you were here, that you'd enjoy the uniqueness of The Winter House like our other, infrequent guests have. But you've managed to disturb the house's balance. For all our sakes, you must leave."

The Housekeeper glared at her. Rebecca was outnumbered, so she went to her room and began packing, imagining the wheezing laughter of the Woodmen coming from the strange, old wallpaper that, she realised now, someone had been so desperate to get rid of.

She didn't have much to pack but wasted time looking for her camera before she remembered that it was with Robert in Room 3. She was thankful to find the corridor empty, although thunder still rumbled along the walls. She found Chalice in the lounge and gave him the key.

"I never meant for any of this to happen," she said. "How could I?"

"It's alright, dear," he said. He sounded frail, nervy. "None of us know what to expect in this place. Once the house settles down perhaps Mr Goodfortune will return. Be careful outside— the path's quite icy now."

It seemed normal to open the door and be faced with snow. Rebecca turned and looked back, just once. Was she abandoning Robert, or was this really the only way to save him? Chalice was already making his way to the back of the house. In his wake, Woodmen squeezed out of the banisters. One gazed at her with unblinking eyes. She put her rucksack on and closed the door.

The ice on the path was slippery so she walked on the snowy grass to the gate. The temperature rose as soon as she got to the road. This, too, felt normal. Despite having spent little time away from The Winter House during her visit, she remembered her way back through the estate. She would go to Pengethon station and take the first train home to London. The sooner she was away, the sooner she could forget this incredible, terrible place and with any luck the dreamlike feeling she'd had since she first saw The Winter House would fade.

The Crossroads of the Four Elements shimmered into view, by the eternally empty playground, taking her by surprise. She was tempted to follow one of the finger posts; if The Winter House lay at the beginning of the road to Aer, who knew what lay further on, and along the other routes? Robert had hinted that all the places were worth seeing. Instinct told her not to. She was still angry and her pride was hurt. They had called her *commonplace*. Inconsequential. Fuck them. She wasn't wanted here. She turned and walked away, looking at her watch and quickening her pace. A train was due within the hour.

She was noticed by the locals as she went. Partly because they didn't know her, and a stranger is always noticed in a small town, but partly because of the child who tagged along behind. The woman hurried down the road, not once turning around to make sure he was keeping up. The child, however, didn't seem to be concerned; to amuse himself, he jumped onto his hands and kept pace behind her through the windswept streets of the town, all the way to Pengethon station.

Parasomnia

"The topography of a land—any land—can be re-drawn, re-mapped; re-made. Earthquakes and volcanoes change the shape of the surface of the Earth. Dust storms on Mars are so severe they alter the physical landscape. Places, familiar or otherwise, change. Do not, then, assume that the world you see today will necessarily be the world you'll see tomorrow. In life, permanence cannot be guaranteed."

—Tallis Zawn (2 December 1967 – 2 December 2020)

In the last light of the day Sargasso saw the storm's approach. It was from the south, she estimated, although when she got her compass she corrected herself; it was from the south-south-west, blurring the valley, moving steadily towards the house. It erased the westward side of the mountain, and everything else in its path, changing the landscape temporarily. As it closed in on the house she could see how heavy the rain was, and knew she should make sure all the windows were shut before it hit, but was transfixed.

Rain suddenly hammered on the window, the wind buffeting and rattling the house. Nothing was visible beyond the rain running down the glass. She was inside the storm now, enclosed in it, invisible to the outside world. She touched the window, enjoying the cold of the glass. Then the storm passed over. The veil lifted and the last colours of sunset were visible above the mountain. She hurried to the front of the house to see the storm pulling away, heading for the forest that was almost too dark to see. She imagined it being erased forever, the looming trees dissolved by the rain.

The storm returned overnight, thunder rumbling around, nearly but never overhead. It was not enough to wake her fully but inspired a night of bad dreams and semi-wakefulness. She always left the curtains at the back of the house open and so awoke to the morning light. Something was different. She opened the window and leant out. The small garden had been battered by the rainstorm but this was not unusual. Most importantly, the hen house was intact. She looked around the bedroom. All was as it should be. She looked out of the back window again, further this time.

The valley looked smaller. Had there been a landslip? The rain had been heavy but not prolonged; but it was possible.

Later that day she walked to the valley, stumbling at times over the rocky moorland. As she approached she could see the valley was intact. There had been no landslip, then, but the valley was indeed different; it had narrowed. She looked at it in detail through her binoculars. The river that ran through the valley was more confined, closer to the mountain that now stood ominously over it. Was it that the river was wider? Sargasso went closer. The river had not broken its banks. The riverbed was covered but not struggling to cope with the amount of water running over it.

She'd had a bad night. Nightmares. Sargasso's mind had played tricks on her. She paddled at the edge of the river then went home. The icy water on her feet was the best part of the day.

That night she slept more soundly but was woken by thunder again. It rumbled around restlessly for a time then faded into the distance. And Sargasso slept, and dreamt of being a stone on the riverbed, looking up at the sky.

The valley was narrower still and this time she was sure of it. After a third stormy night she had returned to the mouth of the valley. This time she was there before sunrise. The sky was moonless but the stars provided enough light to walk by. As the Sun rose behind her she made her way along the valley. This time there was no mistake; the stream was almost hemmed in now between the mountain and the low fells that ran alongside its opposite bank. She spent the day walking the area, both up close and at a distance from the valley. By dusk she had come to the most frightening of conclusions.

The mountain had moved.

The mountain had moved quite noticeably towards the west. By the time Sargasso returned home she had no doubt of it and from the back of the house it was clearly visible. But why? How? Sargasso knew little about geology, but it seemed to her that the only event that could

move a mountain so quickly was a huge earth-
quake, which had clearly not occurred. The rum-
blings she'd heard at night, which she'd assumed
was thunder, had not involved the ground shaking. The valley and the surrounding area was
undamaged, apart from the valley's new de-
creased width. The land on the eastern side of
the mountain, underneath its original position,
was most curious; Sargasso had walked around
the bottom of it, expecting to see huge rifts in the
ground but it, too, was intact, as if the mountain
had never been there. Now she studied it again
through her binoculars. It was a peaceful scene.
A herd of Ibex crossed the enlarged grasslands
to the east, heading for the mountain's crags and
outcrops. The world seemed to be happy with
the mountain in its new position.

Later that day she found her maps of the
area and marked on them, as accurately as she
could, the new information. The mountain had
moved approximately one and a half kilometres
west. She sketched its new position on a separate
sheet of paper, to act as a revised section of her
OS map. She had no surveying equipment, so
was limited in terms of how technically correct
she could be, but as with the map, the sheet was
as accurate as possible in the circumstances.
Sargasso put down her papers and looked out of
the window, as if the answer might be written in
the landscape. Her face, reflected in the glass, was
pale and sickly, something that rarely changed
however much time she spent outside. She left
the maps on the table, along with the ruler and
compass. They would need refining.

First light the next day revealed the moun-

tain had blocked the view of the valley completely, having moved approximately another one hundred and fifty metres to the west, by Sargasso's
calculations. Would the contours, the dimensions,
of the mountain have changed? If its position in
relation to the passage of the Sun had altered,
even by a few degrees—and Sargasso couldn't
believe that it hadn't, even if she couldn't see
it—wouldn't it have an effect on the mountain's
flora and fauna, as well as the land around it? She
picked up one of the hens and held it to her. They,
at least, seemed unaffected by the changes.

Sargasso headed into the forest. The mountain
would not be visible from there. She needed to
get away from it for a while. For two weeks now
she had barely slept; either she was being woken
by the rumbling of the mountain shifting position
or she was unable to go to sleep, anticipating its
movement. And each morning she could only
guess where the mountain would be. After its
initial westerly movement, when she had been
able to predict its path and distance, it had become
entirely unpredictable. On successive days it had
moved in random directions and distance, even
turning *widdershins* a hundred degrees so that
she saw a different face of the mountain from the
house that was itself changing, becoming filled
with her revised maps, notes and charts. Now
amongst the trees, she felt unburdened. Whilst the
forest often made her feel hemmed in, on this day
the trees were protectors, barring the mountain's
way. Sitting on a fallen trunk, all that could be
heard was birdsong, all that could be smelled
was mud and fungus. She closed her eyes, lost in

the moment. When she opened them, there was movement in the trees. She was no longer alone.

A light. Flickering, orange-red. A flaming shape raced between the trees. Sargasso stood up. Was it heading for her? From a distance it looked like a cartwheel but as it got close it changed shape, appearing to be a thing running on four legs. It passed her at tremendous speed. A hot wind blew across her face despite the shape being some yards away. As it disappeared into the denser part of the forest Sargasso noted the ground, usually damp with moss and leaf litter, was scorched where the thing had passed. It did not re-appear and to Sargasso's relief did not set the forest on fire. Was this bizarre phenomena connected to the mountain's movement? It was too much of a coincidence not to be. Sargasso wondered if it was also an omen. But of what, she couldn't guess.

The hens were still laying. The mountain was moving north now and was the closest it had ever been, close enough to throw late afternoon shadows over the garden, something the hens had not experienced before, but they continued as normal. Sargasso, unable to do more than track the mountain's irrational movements, found comfort in the hens' nonchalance. She had become more anxious lately, afraid that the house would be crushed underneath the mountain one night. If she could find out why the mountain was moving she was sure she would find its route and ultimate destination. And the only way she could think of to do that was to be on it when it moved.

~

She had climbed the mountain before and it had been a tiring but enjoyable three hours' walk. This time it felt like a scientific exercise, with the results being critical. She had once read that reaching a mountain's peak was not important in itself—what mattered was becoming *part* of the mountain, not conquering it. This was more relevant to her now. To understand the mountain, what it was doing and why, would help her far more than arrogantly proclaiming to have bested it.

The Ibex had created tracks leading up the mountain and she followed them where she could. Where they had climbed impossible crags she found other, easier routes, still faintly marked on her map from her last ascent, so she made good time. Near the summit she stopped to look up at a jagged crag; a long-horned, bearded Ibex goat peered back at her. She found a boulder with a smooth indentation in it like an ancient throne and she rested on it for a while. She hadn't noticed it before but now she felt welcomed by it. It was a good sign. Breathing deeply, she caught the scent of a dozen different flowers growing nearby.

What would it be like to be one of those flowers? To be the boulder she was sitting on, or the mountain itself, to know its reasons for moving? After some food and water, she climbed the short distance to the summit and looked back to the house. It was reassuring. Taking her map and compass from her bag, she carefully marked the current position of the mountain. Although, she acknowledged, this trip was as much about why as where and how.

Sargasso wondered, too, about the geology of the mountain. Did certain types of rock have weaknesses, a propensity for shifting? Even if that were so, surely nothing was naturally capable of this amount of movement? Sargasso placed her hands on the ground, knowing there was limestone beneath but had a mental image of heat far below, so extreme that the rock had metamorphosed into something else so advanced that it could move great distances without disturbing the area surrounding it.

As the afternoon drifted into evening, Sargasso became calmer. It was cool on the mountain. After a few hours of physical contact with it, she felt she had absorbed some of its essence. Whatever was happening was not malevolent. It was a super-natural phenomenon; the mountain had no control over where it was going and it certainly didn't know why it was going there. There was enormous movement occurring inside it and Sargasso felt as if she was atop a sleeping beast. The Ibex herd joined her on the summit at dusk then disappeared over the sheerest side of the mountain.

Sargasso awoke in the dead of night. The rumbling that had awoken her on so many nights was now more felt than heard. The mountain shook, hard enough for Sargasso to clutch at one of the stone monoliths—natural, she knew, despite their resemblance to human-made sacred sites—that looked at if it was growing from the ground. And then—movement. With a massive effort the mountain pulled away from its position. It was too dark to see what direction the movement was in and besides, Sargasso was too terrified to do anything but hang on as the mountain made its way to only God knew where.

When the movement stopped she slept again and woke up as the Sun rose. With her map and compass she tried to make sense of where the mountain now was.

It had turned 50 degrees clockwise. As to where it had moved to, she went around the edge of the summit and got her bearings.

The mountain had moved almost a kilometre south and was now deeply entrenched in the valley, crushing the fells on either side. Sargasso couldn't see the river but guessed it would be completely blocked and trying to find a new course. She made her way down as quickly as she could, although she was careful to check for subsidence and other damage that might have been sustained with its movements. Every footstep, however, was solid, every rock still firmly in place.

Making her way around the bottom of the mountain she soon saw that the river, completely blocked as she had feared, was already beginning to flood the moorland between the valley and home. Sargasso could only hope that the mountain moved again that night and cleared the river's path. She guessed it would take several days for the river to back up as far as the house, but she was not sure—if the mountain could betray the laws of physics, could the river do so, too? She used the rocks and the thicker tufts of heather to walk on until she reached dry ground and the house. She let the hens out, then sat on the back step, made new sketches and notes and tried to analyse her findings. She could still find no pattern in direction or distance, although the mountain didn't seem to be shifting more than a kilometre at a time. If Sargasso believed in such things she could imagine the huge hand of a god playing with the mountain for its own amusement.

Her map showed a chaotic series of lines. Viewed from above, she again tried to find patterns—meaning—in the lines. But given the chaotic nature of nature, she thought, why should she be able to see the order in what the mountain was doing? Over the next three days Sargasso noted the water level as it crept closer to the house. At its closest point—the mouth of the valley—the river was a kilometre away. It skirted wide to the east before looping north-west and cutting through the far edge of the forest. The nights were silent, which should have been a blessing but it was a disastrous silence, and so Sargasso got no more sleep than usual. With the area around the house becoming boggy, and Sargasso seriously considering keeping the hens inside the house, it was with great relief that she woke up on the third night to the sound of distant rumbling. For the first time she didn't worry about where the mountain was going; it would be allowing the river to return to its normal course. The house and the land around it was safe. She drifted back to sleep and the rumbling drifted away.

Four kilometres south and then three kilometres east. This was how far the mountain had moved during the night. Sargasso was observing its new position from the battered fells aligning the valley. It had taken some time to find the mountain and she had imagined it simply having vanished, before spotting it, away from the southern end of the valley.

One of the things that mystified Sargasso most was the land underneath the mountain's original position.

It was undamaged.

Whereas the fells—and the river—showed the effects of the mountain's movement, the land which Sargasso thought would reflect the disaster that had struck it had been instantly reclaimed by nature. Grasses, heather and gorse covered the land, which was only as rough and rutted as the rest of the moorland in the area. Studying the area in more detail, Sargasso found insects and spiders inhabited it as much as elsewhere. Now standing on a fell that would carry its scars for years, Sargasso realised that she had been right to compare the mountain to a sleeping beast, had perhaps not even gone far enough, for the land was surely as alive as she was.

She shook her head and updated her notes and the OS map; it was important to keep her studies as scientific as possible. Romantic notions about the mountain were only distracting her.

That night she slept soundly, or thought she had, although it was still dark when she awoke. To her relief, it was quiet. She squinted to see the time. It was 8 a.m.. She went to the kitchen, switched on the light and went outside. The house, the garden and a little of the land around it was surrounded by rock. She grabbed her torch from the kitchen, went back outside and trained it on the rock, following it upwards to a ceiling that was an almost perfect dome. She ran out of the garden and felt the wall to make sure it was real. It was solid; cold and dripping wet in places. Underneath her bare feet the moor had also given way to rock.

The mountain had moved again — this time to cover the house. But instead of being crushed as Sargasso had feared, the house was intact, somewhere inside the mountain. She was aware of air blowing gently over her face and made her way around the chamber, looking for a possible way out, but could see nothing bigger than a small fissure.

She let the hens out and fed them. They scratched and pecked their way about, seemingly at ease with their new surroundings, and it was only then that she realised that she, too, had quickly become unconcerned. In fact, there was something reassuring about it. And after all, the mountain would move again soon.

Over the course of the next two days Sargasso explored the chamber as fully as she was able. It was possible, using a ladder, to climb almost halfway up the wall. A number of ledges, almost invisible from ground level, were accessible using the ladder, two of which led away, further into the mountain. Sargasso found little in the first passageway but the second was more interesting. She played the torchlight over the walls, stopping at some strange marks. Scratches, perhaps. She brushed a finger over them. They were lines, in a faint but deep and definite red. Cave paintings? Someone had been here at some point in time. She stooped and made her way further along the passageway. There was a breath of air. She breathed it in and pointed the torch dead ahead. The passageway ended. And yet it didn't. What was clearly once a back wall had a narrow fissure in it, perhaps just big enough for her to squeeze through. When she felt its edges her fingers came away dusty. The rock appeared to have been chiselled away, relatively recently.

Below the slit was debris from the hole. Sargasso picked up one of the bigger pieces. She was looking for evidence of human activity but this was even more intriguing. There was a scattering of bones all over the back of the passageway. She brushed the stones and dust aside to reveal a skeletal bird's wing, stretched out as if in flight. Other bones lay nearby, some big enough to possibly be human. A large skull, impossible to age, lay right in the opening. Sargasso picked it up, meaning to take it with her, but something—superstition?—held her back. Instead she took notes: long and thin, it was 28cm in length and 16cm wide, with large, widely-placed eye sockets and a trunk-like nose bone. Its teeth did not fit together at all, but vied for space like irregular spikes in the animal's jaw. She put the stone she had originally picked up into her bag, and retreated.

Now she was able to map the inside, as well as the outside of the mountain. Her compass showed that the house was facing due south as it always had, so she assumed it hadn't been moved by the activities of the mountain. She estimated the chamber's ceiling was around 17 metres high. Despite her first impression, the dome was not perfectly circular and so she mapped the chamber's internal contours as well as she could and was careful to note that their heights were from the chamber's floor, rather than sea level. Without sight of the sky she referred to her watch to ascertain whether it was light or dark outside. She wondered what it would be like to take the watch off and lose all sense of whereabouts in the day she was. Perhaps the hens would have a more instinctive grasp of whether it was day or night. Or perhaps they would all go insane. She decided not to take any risks and kept to her normal schedule.

The familiarity she felt in her surroundings seeped through to her dreams. For two nights she dreamt of living in the chamber, using passageways that criss-crossed the mountain's interior. The dreams were brief, like flashbacks of a previous life. Or the ghosts of someone else's memory. And in the mornings she looked at her complexion — the palest white, as it had always been — and wondered for a moment whether the inside of the mountain had once been her home.

She checked the generator several times over the course of the two days. Unhampered as she was by her enclosure, she was grateful to have a working power supply; pitch darkness or weak light from her fading torch was not something she relished. She had no water supply but plenty in the water butts. But she couldn't work out how the house hadn't been crushed. So little of what was happening made sense. It was difficult to remain scientific about it.

On the third night flames cut through the darkness. Sargasso, determined to stay awake each night until the mountain moved away from the house, was falling asleep when she noticed the flickering light.

The shapeshifting creature had returned. She opened the window and watched. It bowled along the floor of the chamber, uncurling its legs as it reached the garden. It raced around the back of the house, leaving pockets of flames in its wake, then circled the house, more slowly this time. Sargasso got the impression it was looking for something. As it approached the hen house on its circuit it changed direction and climbed skilfully up to one of the ledges. It lit the passageway as it entered and Sargasso recognised it as the passageway where the bones and the fissure had been. The flames died down and faded from sight. Sargasso leaned further out of the window but there was nothing more to be seen. She should go up there and see whether the creature had died, or, as she suspected, it had slipped into the crevice at the back of the passageway and was now making its way out of the mountain. She should follow it, but sleep was claiming her and instead she staggered back to bed.

Sargasso awoke to light so painfully intense that she was sure the flaming creature was in the room with her.

It was sunlight. The mountain had moved.

The fresh air was glorious. Sargasso breathed deeply as she walked around the house, following the scorch marks left by the flaming creature. When she got to the front she once again observed the altered landscape.

The mountain had swallowed up most of the forest. Of course it could have crushed the trees under its mass of limestone but Sargasso suspected some of the forest at least was intact, housed in chambers like the one she had been in.

She spent the day working in the garden, not having time until the evening to make notes about the latest movement. But as she wrote, she finally began to see the importance of having documented the whole event so thoroughly. The landscape was being rewritten, and she was there to record it.

But only momentarily.

It would be something to leave behind, then.

The watching, the note-taking, the speculation, however, was not enough. She had a hundred theories but no evidence to support any of them. All she had was a living piece of the land moving, separating itself from everything around it. To fully understand it she would have to return, not just to the mountain, but to its interior, and truly become part of it.

If the flaming creature had got out, then there was a way in.

The next morning Sargasso set the hens free, scattering their food around the area. Their flight feathers were almost healed, so they had a chance in the wild. She took some provisions but little else; life inside the mountain would be very different. She would be very different; if the land was subject to change then so was she. Unable to fully relinquish her old life, however, she put her house key in her pocket without really being aware she had done so.

She approached the mountain from what was left of the forest. The lower slopes were in shade, concealing her almost completely as, step by step, the land absorbed her.

We are all Falling Towards the Centre of the Earth

Located as it was on the outskirts of Freiburg, the *bierhaus* was used to welcoming strangers, usually hikers, who had journeyed through the Black Forest and wanted refreshment before going to their accommodation in the town. The woman who arrived that afternoon was different. She carried a small bag and a big walking stick but was not dressed for walking. Or for anything else; her clothes were virtually rags. Her skin, brown from being outdoors, was heavily lined with age. She was, the landlord guessed, at least seventy years old. Alone, she walked in and took a seat at a table and looked at the landlord.

"I have no money," she said, in a quiet, heavy voice. "But I am happy to work for a meal and a beer or two, if you please."

The woman's honesty impressed the landlord and he filled a glass and bought it to her table.

"This one is on me," he said. "I will think about the rest of it. Tell me, have you come far?"

The old woman took a long drink. "I have come a long way in kilometres, but in every other sense, I'm afraid, very little distance indeed," she said. "I believe I've been walking for forty-three years."

There was a murmur from the handful of other drinkers and the landlord raised his eyebrows.

"To have been inspired to such a journey must have taken a monumental event. It must be worth a meal and a drink—and a bed for the night—to hear your story."

So, over a meal of meat and cheese and soup, she told them her tale.

"My name is Ursula. My life, until the age of 27, was of no great consequence. It was 1967 and I lived alone in an apartment near Oberhof on the shores of the magnificent Jungfernsee lake. My neighbours were good people but I was lonely. It is not always enough to have good conversation with someone but to end the evening alone in one's bed, is it? But otherwise life was good enough.

"And then things changed."

"Stop pulling the lead, Friedrich, there's a good boy," said Ursula. She enjoyed walking the dog, which belonged to King Leopold, a bed-ridden neighbour, but knew she had no authority over him. The lake was irresistable and he grunted and pulled again.

Someone was lying on the little beach. On a summer evening it would not be unusual but this was a cold night and the figure wasn't moving. A shiver crossed Ursula. She had never seen death at close quarters.

Crossing herself, she went closer. There were drag marks on the sand, indicating that the poor wretch had crawled out of the lake.

It was a woman. Her skin was dark, almost jet black. She lay on her stomach, weighed down by something—clothes?—piled on her back. Ursula went closer and touched the woman's hand. It was cold. But it moved, twisting to grasp her hand. The woman took a gasping lungful of air. And Ursula cried with joy, happy that she wasn't holding the hand of a corpse.

She wrapped her coat around the woman, who was shivering violently, and took her home, Friedrich trotting beside her co-operatively. Ursula tried not to panic but was aware of how dangerous the woman's situation—and, by association, her own—might be. She had no possessions with her and if she was carrying identity papers in a pocket they'd have been ruined in the water. But first of all she needed a bath and dry clothing and, probably, a doctor. Her doctor was a kind man. He might not ask questions. She talked to the woman on the way, hoping it would reassure her, but not knowing if the woman understood a word she was saying.

By the time they got home the woman seemed a little better. She even spoke.

"Thank you. Thank you. I would have died of cold if I'd lain there all night," she said, in perfect but hesitant German. Ursula put the kettle on, quickly returned Friedrich to his master and reappeared in the lounge.

To find her guest, having stripped off her clothes, in the process of unfurling the pair of wings that lay upon her back.

She stood, wings open, looking like Christ upon the cross.

"They're so heavy when they're wet," she said, a slight smile on her face.

After she had drunk tea and bathed — with Ursula preparing it and finding clothes in a dreamlike state — the woman, whose name was Kol, let Ursula study her wings in detail.

The feathers were a deep, dark blue, with lines of grey running through them. The texture, light but incredibly strong, felt pleasing to Ursula's fingers. Bones, thin as wire, ran along the top. Each wing was at least 90 centimetres long and perhaps half of that at their widest point. They were attached to Kol's shoulder blades by a muscular joint.

If she had thought it a strange joke, she was mistaken. The wings were real.

Ursula had a Winged Woman in her home. And what's more, one with no papers.

Ursula had to work the next day and left Kol, who had insisted that a doctor wasn't required, at home to rest. When Ursula got home she found Kol dressed and wanting to see the outside world. She had adapted Ursula's shirt so that she could wear it back to front and could button it around her wings. Together they walked down to the lake. Ursula was immensely curious as to where Kol came from and how she had come to be in the lake but was aware that, as with so many things, the less one knew the safer one was. Her interest in the Winged Woman overcame her caution, however, and she asked Kol where her home was.

Kol looked towards the south. "The mountains, a day's flight from here. We've been there for centuries."

Ursula was surprised, pleased and uneasy to hear that Kol was not unique. "There are more of you?"

"Like me but not like me. I have wings but no fur to protect against the snow and ice. Some of us are lucky enough to have both."

"And how did you come to be in the lake? Do you often fly over here?"

Kol's brow furrowed. "I don't remember what made me fall back to Earth. Or how I didn't drown. I just remember you touching my hand."

Ursula blushed. There was so much more she wanted to know but where to begin? She hoped there would be time to find out more.

They walked alongside the lake for a while. Every now and then Kol would adjust the coat Ursula had given her. It covered her wings but was clearly uncomfortable.

Kol thought hard before she spoke again. "Tomorrow, before it gets light, I will fly home. I want to thank you for all your kindness."

"You don't have to go yet," said Ursula. "It's no imposition for you to stay a while longer."

While it would be safer for both of them if Kol left, Ursula was disappointed. The Winged Woman was a new friend, and they were hard to come by.

It was dusk when they returned to the apartment block. Once in the lobby, Kol shrugged off the jacket. Ursula looked on, horrified, as a group of her neighbours appeared from the stairway. The five of them stared at Kol's dark skin then, as she turned away, they gasped.

They headed towards Horst's apartment on the ground floor. He managed to unlock his door, despite having eyes only for Kol's incredible wings. Ursula grabbed Kol's hand and pushed them all inside.

The five neighbours—two elderly couples, Ilse and Gunter and Gerhard and Hildegard, and the widower Horst—milled around for a while before Horst, who hated untidyness, pointed people towards chairs. Only Ursula and Kol, who were too jittery to sit, were left standing.

There was an expectant silence.

"This is Kol. A friend of mine," said Ursula.

"She has wings on her back," Gerhard pointed out.

"Is she an Angel?" shouted Ilse, who was given to over-reaction.

"Don't be ridiculous," chided Hildegard. "There are no such things as Angels. She is a Winged Woman."

Kol grinned. "Have you met one of my kind before?" she asked hopefully.

"Never!" Hildegard was forceful. "But at my age one has learnt that not everything in this world has been found and labelled and written down in a book."

"This is blasphemous," said Ilse.

"This could be treason!" said Horst, not wanting to be overlooked. They was, after all, in his apartment. "Do the authorities know of her? Do they approve?"

Ursula turned on him. "Kol nearly drowned in the lake last night. She'll be leaving the country before daybreak. Would you like to explain everything to the authorities and be treated like a lunatic?"

Ursula took Kol home. Not only was the Winged Woman leaving—presumably never to return—but there might be an official knock at her door to boot.

She was tired but determined not to sleep and waste the time she had left with Kol. They talked about their lives for hours. Ursula felt hers was dull in comparison, but Kol was fascinated. Life in the mountains was equally easier and more difficult than here in the East, but both their lives revolved around their own ways of survival. Surviving the weather and finding enough to eat was primarily Kol's life, and there were disputes between the tribes of Winged People at times, but when those things were taken care of, there was pleasure.

"We fly. We soar around the mountains and through the passes. The wind takes us wherever it pleases. Sometimes I never want to land. But gravity always wins."

People—ordinary humans—sometimes climbed the mountains or travelled through the passes. Over the years some had spied a glimpse, no more, of the Winged People, tales they'd returned home with that had passed into folklore, not dismissed but not believed either. Some of the Winged People ventured further afield, flying over human habitations. Kol had often done so, fascinated by the light and movement below. She was confident and strong in the air—how she had come to fall into the Jungfernsee was a mystery to her.

For Ursula, life was far more banal. She

always had enough food to eat and, while she shivered through the winters, there was little chance of freezing to death. Her real hardship was in not knowing who she could trust, and on the petty restrictions on life. Her people were unable to spread their wings; flying was strictly forbidden. Each imagined the other's life as full of mystery and excitement. By the time dawn was approaching they had fallen asleep on Ursula's bed. Kol awoke with a start, but the timing was perfect. First light was just beginning to take the edge off the darkness. She would be able to see her way but was unlikely to be seen amongst the cumulus scattered across the sky. Kol wanted to leave from the beach where she had been found, but Ursula was worried that any delay would mean more chance of being discovered, so they stood at the back of the apartment block. They said their goodbyes amongs the washing lines and bins.

"This feels like a dream," said Ursula, tightly clasping Kol's hand.

"This is stranger than my dreams," said Kol. She looked up at the sky, the half-Moon lighting the clouds moving south-east, the wind favourable for her flight home.

Ursula gasped when Kol unfurled her wings, the most natural and beautiful things in the world. The wings moved with enormous power, sending a chill wind through Ursula's hair. Kol rose off the ground then landed heavily with a cry of pain. One wing, clearly damaged, hung towards the floor. With Ursula's help Kol was able to re-fold it. Kol sat on the ground, wracked with pain and frustration. The wing was more damaged than she'd realised. Going home was, for now at least, impossible.

"You need to see a doctor," said Ursula. Or would a veterinary surgeon be better, bearing in mind where Kol's injury was? They decided on a doctor. Doctor Ernst had seen the tenants through all kinds of ailments. Ursula thought— hoped—he could be trusted. Ursula tried to get Kol back to her apartment unseen, but Ilse and Gunter appeared with Friedrich on an early walk.

"Have you not ascended to Heaven yet?" screeched Ilse. Even Gunter, who was going deaf, winced.

"One of my wings is a little damaged," whispered Kol. "I'll be gone soon, I promise."

Gunter turned to Ursula as they passed. "We'll keep this to ourselves. Don't worry," he said, in a conspiratorial hiss.

Not for the first time, Ursula wondered what her neighbours' past was. They'd spoken of the war, naturally, but not in detail. It was best not to know the parts individuals had played. It was history. Her thoughts returned to Kol; a mixture of concern for the Winged Woman's wellbeing and relief that she hadn't left. Kol had been able to get a short way off the ground. Surely her wing couldn't be that badly damaged?

The Doctor arrived later that day. Kol had been resting and was in better spirits. Doctor Ernst was fifty-six years old and had seen many injuries but the woman—the stranger—who sat before him now was truly unique. He had baulked when she'd turned and shown him her wings. He wondered why Ursula, a perfectly reasonable woman in his experience, would play such a trick on him. He baulked again when he realised the wings were real. He drank the strong coffee Ursula had placed on the table and tried to gather his thoughts.

"Are you registered with the practice, young lady?" he asked. Something ordinary, orderly, was the best he could come up with.

Kol looked quizzical.

"She's here by accident. Temporarily. As soon as she's well enough she's leaving," said Ursula.

"This is all extremely unorthodox," said the doctor. Then, to Kol, "If your wing is injured, perhaps I'm not the person to help. I deal with... human problems."

"It is skin and bone and muscle," said Kol. "Please help me."

Ursula sat next to the doctor. "You might be the only doctor in the world who's ever seen such a thing. This is a unique case for you."

"One I can never tell anyone about," replied Ernst.

"But one day—who knows? It's still a historic case."

Ernst finished his drink. "My job is to heal the sick. And I realise this is a delicate case that could be *misunderstood*. So I'll do my best."

With her wings outstretched, Kol was an incredible sight, taking up much of the space in Ursula's lounge. Taking extreme care, Ernst examined the area where Kol felt the most pain. Pushing the feathers aside, he found some deep lacerations. They didn't look infected, but the patient would need antibiotics. The wing was primarily constructed of thin, fragile feeling bones not dissimilar to a human arm. One of which was clearly fractured in several places, judging by the pain Kol was in when he touched them.

Before he gave his diagnosis, the doctor excused himself and went to the bathroom, where he wept briefly. The enormity of what he was dealing with was overwhelming. When he returned he prepared a syringe and tried to steady his nerves and his voice.

"I have no knowledge of your physiology, Fraulein Kol, so I can only hope that what I prescribe will do you no harm, so be vigilant for side effects. I'm going to give you some antibiotics for the cuts on your wing. You have several fractures in the bones there, too. No open fractures, thankfully, but they will take time to heal. You could do with having an x-ray on that wing, and the wounds stitched up, but obviously it would be unwise to go to the hospital. We will have to hope for the best."

After some indecision, he administered the injection. That done, Ursula opened her door to let the doctor out and discovered a cake on her doorstep. Looking up and down the corridor, she saw Hildegard spying from the safety of her door.

"Did you make this?"

Hildegard said nothing as Doctor Ernst walked away then hurried to Ursula's door, grabbed the cake from the floor and strode inside.

Gunter, then, had not kept his word.

The three of them had coffee and cake. It had a strange, delicate flavour, reminiscent of cloves. Hildegard announced that it was a

Dianthus cake.

Kol started.

"That's an Alpine flower," she said. "This is the sort of thing my mother would have made. I thought it was familar. How did you know?"

"I didn't. I just thought you might like something to remind you of the Alps. How badly are you injured?"

Ursula left them to talk. She went to her balcony for some air. There was no possibility of keeping Kol under wraps for several weeks. It was natural for people to be curious, but it would only take one telephone call to put Kol in deadly danger. The authorities would not recognise the likes of Kol. Ursula suspected even the West would react harshly to the Winged Woman. Hildegard meant well—the old woman, a grandmother and a midwife before her retirement—was full of caring. While Ilse and Horst couldn't see past the fact that Kol had wings, Hildegard only saw a person far from home and in pain. Nothing else mattered. Ursula returned to the lounge. Kol, eyes shining, was regaling their guest with descriptions of home.

"The thing is," Ursula interrupted, "even if Kol never leaves the apartment, too many people know she's here. It's dangerous."

"No one here would report her!" Hildegard exclaimed. "Well. Perhaps someone would. Appearances can be deceptive; not everyone is what they seem."

Ursula was dreaming of flying. Her beautiful, powerful wings carried her easily. Higher and faster she went. Over the lake, futher and further, to the mountains, with their summer meadows at the foothills and snow capping the peaks. Her speed and height made her nauseous but the experience was euphoric and she couldn't stop. And there, on a sharply angled ridge, stood Kol, arms and wings outstretched, ready to greet her. Ursula landed, grateful that the flight was over. In the distance she heard the cry of a baby, although no other Winged People were visible. As she went to fold up her wings, she realised to her dismay that they were no longer there. She heard Kol's voice.

"We are all slaves to our physical selves," she said.

As the weeks passed, Kol gradually became more visible to the tenants of the apartment block. Since it was clearly impossible to Ilse and Gunter to have kept such a secret, Ursula surmised that keeping Kol out of sight would only arouse even more suspicion amongst her neighbours. It was dangerous—Ursula didn't know everyone in the block, so could not guess where their loyalties lay but Hildegard and Gerhard had lived there for decades and knew everyone. And while that did not mean that some of the tenants didn't have some unpleasant secrets the couple—as trusted as anyone could be—would hopefully talk any unsympathetic neighbours around. There was no open hostility towards Kol and as the weeks passed and there was no knock at the door. Ursula hoped it meant everyone was happy.

Two people, however, were not.

Horst was grappling with a dilemma. He had been born in the previous century, and that was where he most felt at home. He'd fought and to his surprise survived two world wars. There had been so many changes in his lifetime, so much worry. Sometimes to still the anxiety he played music; one classical piece in one room, a different piece in the other. Where the two met would be a beautiful blend, a third piece—not chaos as one would assume. These days things were easier. He liked the order that life in the GDR gave him. Everything that was done was to keep them safe. And now that safety was being threatened. He had met Kol several times and there seemed to be nothing threatening about her, but she was just so *unorthodox*. He had almost got used to the Turks living in the town, although their ways were strange enough. They at least had papers. Kol's skin was savagely dark, she had no authorisation to be here and those frightful wings were made for trouble. They were the sort of thing the West might use to allow strange people to spy on him.

Hildegard's unhappiness was for different reasons. It was not the safety of the country she worried about. They were all in danger because of Kol's presence. If the authorities discovered her, all the tenants would be penalised for having harboured her. But Kol would present them with a particular problem. One that would be dealt with in the harshest possible way. After all, once the good citizens of the GDR had seen a Winged Woman, they might all want wings and how could security be guaranteed in that case?

For Hildegard, Kol was like censored music; a glimpse of something *more*. Colour in a monochrome life.

Hildegard was nearly as old as Horst but her experiences had given her a different view of the world. She had delived many new lives, many of them happy events but many tragedies too, babies too sick to live, babies born into despairing homes too poor to feed them.

And one baby who had been born with wings.

It had been during the Great War, when she had just qualified as a midwife. Thankfully the birth had been straightforward. Hildegard, all nerves, had silently thanked God for such an easy delivery. She was drying the boy off and went to wipe away the blood and mucus from his back when she realised that tiny grey wings were underneath. Staggered, she wiped them as clean as she could. The boy was otherwise perfectly healthy. The mother was too elated and exhausted to talk but her sisters were present and took Hildegard aside.

"We were afraid this would be the case," they said. "So many have died in this terrible war. Such destruction. Can you see it in your heart to let this baby boy go unreported?"

"But how did it happen?" Hildegard was almost as shocked at the sisters' lack of surprise as she had been at the sight of the wings.

"Tilda went away for a while," said one. "A month or two, no more. Where she went or how she got there she never said, but when she returned to the village she was full of strange stories. It was as if she had been in a dream. She talked of people who flew among the mountains, who lived in caves and sometimes flew over our homes."

"At first we thought she was suffering from a fever," said the other. "But there was such detail! And when it became clear she was pregnant, we began to think the unthinkable. But it isn't that beautiful baby boy's fault. We can look after him together if we're left in peace to do so."

Hildegard collected her things in silence. She had done her job well; baby and mother were healthy and happy. Anything else was not her business, she told herself. She came to terms with the incident by choosing to believe that the boy had suffered a unique physical deformity. And now, all these years later, here was Kol. Which meant that, wherever it was that she came from, might be the man that baby boy grew up to be. And that he had been born precisely the way he was supposed to be.

Kol was healing. Ursula was rigorous in cleaning the lacerations on her wing and there was no sign of infection. The fractures were slower to heal. Kol could almost open her wings fully without experiencing too much pain, but anything more than their slight movement was not possible. As the weather was warm, she often went to the lake to feel its cool breeze. Ursula would accompany her as often as she could, helping Kol by throwing sand over her wings to keep mites and other parasites at bay. Kol loved the dragonflies; their beautiful metallic colours that glinted in the sun, the snapping sound their wings made when they passed close by. Kol seemed more settled now, less keen to leave. Ursula wondered what that meant. After two months she knew she was in love with Kol, although naturally she hadn't declared it, but one unseasonably cold night Kol had offered to keep her warm and by dawn they had become lovers. Ursula now led a bizarre double life; as a quiet, ordinary, loyal Government clerk and in her forbidden, unorthodox life with Kol. She could give neither up.

Kol's memory was healing, too. The horror of being underwater, almost drowning in the lake before dragging herself ashore, had erased the memory of how she had got there. Now it was returning, in dreams.

Something had been hovering over the exact centre of the lake. A force so overwhelming her strong wings couldn't fight it. In her dreams a translucent, taloned eagle's claw grabbed her and threw her down into the lake.

And one morning, after one of these dreams, she woke up and knew what had caused her to fall from the sky.

It was gravity. The overwhelming force of the Universe, somehow stronger in this quiet patch of Germany, had plucked her from the sky and nearly caused her to drown.

King Leopold was entertaining guests.

His apartment had been slightly rearranged for the occasion. Bed-ridden these last thirteen years, his bed usually sat in the lounge, by the window. For this gathering, however, he had instructed Claude, his carer, to move the bed to the centre of the room. From this position he was able to command everyone's attention.

Hildegard snorted. "Look at the King holding court! His throne's beginning to look shabby. Perhaps it should have stayed by the window."

She had a love/hate relationship with Leopold. As did many of the tenants. Some were inclined to listen to the nonsense he came out with, which usually consisted of who he'd most like to put to the sword if he were king. Who had first nicknamed him King Leopold was long since forgotten, but the comparison with the appalling King of Belgium was not entirely humourous. His dog Friedrich on his lap, he was pontificating about the laziness of the modern worker. Much to everyone except Gunter's amusement, Ilse stepped in and interrupted the monologue.

"Come now, Leopold! We all know you could walk if you wanted to. You are the laziest of the lazy!"

He suspected she was joking but nevertheless foamed at the mouth in outrage that she could be saying such a thing at his party.

Ursula and Kol sat unobtrusively in a corner. Ursula used to love these occasions but felt anxious for Kol. Kol stretched her wings every so often and even gave them a flap. Each time she did it everyone looked. Was it in simple curiosity, or anger? King Leopold, Ursula noticed, appeared oblivious to Kol's presence. He had objected to her when she'd first walked into his apartment, several weeks ago now. Unaware then of her wings, her black skin immediately deemed her untrustworthy. She had accompanied Ursula and Friedrich on a walk and was with her as they returned the dog. He had been disappointed with Ursula, having not seen her as that kind of woman and was hissing at her that *that* woman had better not have touched Friedrich with her dirty hands when he saw Kol interacting with the dog and it was clear they adored one another. She treated him with such kindness. It stopped him short. Since then he had been unsure what to think of her. He had seen her wings, of course, but refused to believe in them. It simply wasn't possible, therefore it simply *wasn't*. He complained about her, of course, but mostly to Claude, who shrugged and made noncommittal noises in reply to whatever King Leopold said about her. Or about anything else, for that matter. Not many people tried to argue with the bed-ridden man as he raged about things he knew little about and meted out judgments to people he'd never met. And Claude was an employee, in even less of a position to disagree than King Leopold's neighbours.

So he didn't. And he had no opinion on Kol. He didn't know her, so how could he? It was no matter to him whether or not she had wings. As Ursula looked around the room she caught Claude's eye and gave him a sympathetic smile. His job, after all, was far from easy.

The other tenants—and others in the area, since it had been impossible to expect Kol to remain in the vicinity of the apartment block— had, after initially being suspicious of the sudden arrival of a Winged Woman, gradually accepted her. On the surface, at any rate.

"I wouldn't want to be surrounded by Winged People. I would feel like a stranger in my own home," said the grocery shop cashier to Gerhard one day, "but this woman is polite enough. Does she have papers yet?"

Lack of official approval seemed to be at the crux of any nervousness anyone had about Kol. As things stood, surely they were complicit in the harbouring of an illegal alien? If the authorities would only issue papers to her! It would make everyone's lives much easier.

Kol hadn't flown now for ten weeks. Her bones had healed but her wing muscles needed work to become ready for the journey home.

Home was such a long way away. Kol felt the distance physically and emotionally. She missed the mountains, the clear air, her tribe. Oberhof was flat and its people were ridiculous; anchored to the ground in every way. Ursula was different. She was afraid to dream, as all the people here were, but she did it anyway. Everyone was obsessed with threats, some real but most imagined. They strangled themselves with dangers that weren't there.

Kol's wing could soon be ready for flight but something stopped her from preparing herself properly. She was well aware that her love for Ursula was something else perceived as a threat and Ursula was clearly frightened for both of them.

And Ursula wanted to fly.

They had stood on the rooftop of the apartment block. Everything was grey—the concrete, the clouds, the work clothes Ursula wore. Kol exercised her wings, stretching and easing them around. Ursula watched, entranced by the Winged Woman's movements, forgetting to breathe. She didn't need to breathe. She was entranced by Kol, besotted with her. Was this love or obsession, the kind of thing schoolgirls experience and grow out of? But to say that was to dismiss it. Caring for Kol's wounds had given Ursula an understanding of Kol's wings as well as a fascination with them.

They were superb, a natural work of art. Even though they were not at their best, they remained incredibly powerful.

The joints on Kol's shoulderblades, where her wings were attached, were equally fascinating. Ursula had spent many hours exploring that area of Kol's body. It was not strange or freakish or ugly, just part of a body that was, to all intents and purposes, human. The Winged Woman's toes were long and had great dexterity, to make landing on unstable surfaces safer; to Ursula's delight they gripped her hand with outrageous strength. Now, as Kol beat her wings, a single feather floated away and made its way to the rooftop. Ursula picked it up. It was solid, heavy. She put it in her pocket.

When she looked up Kol was rising into the air. She didn't go far, as the damaged wing wasn't capable of proper flight, but it was enough to make her remember how much she loved to fly. Ursula watched in a mixture of joy and sadness. She wanted to share every part of Kol's life but one thing would always elude her. As Kol landed, elated, Ursula embraced her, and before she could stop them, her heartbreak flooded out.

"I want to fly with you."

She cried then. And was ashamed, for Kol was so happy.

"I wish you could fly, too," she said. "All I can offer you are the mountains. I want you to come with me."

And Ursula, naturally, said yes.

"The southern border is the easiest to cross," said Gerhard eventually.

"You won't be the first we've helped, you

see," said Hildegard. "People think my husband
is a dullard. It suits him that they think that way."

Gerhard laughed. "You have no idea!
The secrets people give away because they
don't believe I'd understand the importance of
what they're saying! A combination of bribery
and incompetence makes it possible to get you
across," he said. "You'll travel from the railway
station in my contact's automobile. He will take
you to Numberg. Then it's up to you."

It would take every penny Ursula had to
get them both to the mountains. She had nothing
to pay Gerhard for his trouble and the risk he
was taking to help them.

"All I want from you," he said, "is your
promise that you'll do your very best to be happy."

The date of travel was two months hence.
It gave Ursula time to earn more money and to
discreetly sell a few of her possessions. All either
of them would need in the mountains was some
clothing. This fact made Ursula look at her things
in a different light; in terms of what was needed
in order to survive, nearly everything she owned
was meaningless. It was also looking considerably
more likely that this would be a one-way trip.
After all, if she was amongst Winged People, in
the highest regions of the Alps, for any length of
time, how could she possibly return, either here
or to the West, where everything was so *flat?*

Horst was still unhappy. It was clear that no
attempt had been made to register the black,
winged female with the authorities. Had such an
attempt been made, he would have known about
it. And so would King Leopold—visits would

have been made to the apartment block, the spies spied upon by the bed-ridden man.

"You would surely be doing your duty if you contacted the authorities," said King Leopold from his usual position, in bed by the window.

"Or you could do *your* duty and contact them," Horst replied. "We are equally responsible, equally culpable."

King Leopold considered this while Horst ranted on. "Neither of us should be in this position. If I had my way the skies themselves would be better patrolled. How is it that a Winged Woman can fly over the Republic unchallenged? The implications for national security are monstrous. Someone's incompetence is to blame."

"It's not that I don't want her here," mused King Leopold. "Friedrich adores her and he is a good judge of character. It is just all so irregular. I have never seen a woman of her kind before; she needs to go through official channels."

Whether King Leopold was referring to Kol's wings or the colour of her skin was unclear, but Horst supposed it did not matter—either way, the woman invited suspicion. He was quiet for some minutes. Then he spoke. "I will take Friedrich for a walk. I think this time we'll go through the centre of town."

King Leopold knew what that meant. The Government buildings were in the centre of town. There might be official visitors to look out for after all.

It was the way he was walking that gave him away. Gerhard passed him in the street and Horst was definitely strutting. It was subtle, but for someone as observant as Gerhard, quite obvious. Enough to make him turn on his heels and hurry home.

Horst looked like a man who had been praised, commended for being a good citizen. Which, as Gerhard was well aware, equated to doing the Government's snooping for them.

"This one has a mixture of Alpine flowers in it," said Hildegard as she passed pieces of cake around. "We've become very partial to it."

"... but you didn't speak to Horst when you saw him?" asked Ursula. "So you can't be sure of what he's done?"

"There's often no need to ask a man a question," said Gerhard. "His manner, his expression, will tell you everything."

"It is better that Horst doesn't know that we know what he's done," said Hildegard. "It will make our plan... less visible."

"And Gerhard has his reputation to uphold," said Kol. She shook her wings a little, making herself more comfortable. "It will be disastrous if people realise how sharp he really is."

Horst had betrayed them. Ursula felt violently ill. Once the authorities had Kol, they would never let her go. Public knowledge of her would cause panic, outrage. It would lower morale. Therefore, Ursula supposed, once she had been wrung of information, she would likely be imprisoned for the rest of her life or quietly done away with, with no one the wiser.

As if this wasn't horrifying enough, Ursula wondered if there would be implications for the Winged People in the mountains. Although the authorities were not known for their imagination;

it was unlikely that they would even consider there could be more than one Winged Woman. No, they would be so obsessed with the theory that the West had fashioned Kol purely to unsettle the Republic that no other thought or other possibility could be entertained. The Winged People in the mountains would be safe. It was only Kol—and herself—who were in danger.

"So!" said Gerhard. "The plan has to be brought forward. I will arrange your transport and you'll leave at the earliest opportunity."

Until then, vigilance would be required. All trace of Kol needed to be wiped from Ursula's apartment for when the authorities inevitably arrived. While it would be impossible to deny that Kol had been there, a distressing story about threats and coercion, and Ursula's innocence, might be enough to keep the authorities at bay until the pair made their escape. Ursula was of loyal character. It would count in her favour. Kol could hide in the basement. It was the best they could do in the circumstances and they would just have to hope for the best.

It hurt to beat her wings enough to get off the ground but Kol was ferocious and let the pain fire her anger. King Leopold was outside enjoying a rare breath of fresh air and a chance to see and criticise new people. He was sitting in a grand chair with Friedrich on his lap. Horst was pacing importantly around, much to King Leopold's annoyance; he couldn't turn around to see him.

Kol couldn't hear their conversation and was glad of it. Only six feet off the ground, she was nevertheless an astounding sight, her wings at full stretch, blocking the sun. She swooped at Horst, shrieking, like a bird harrying a threat to her chick.

King Leopold heard the shrieks and felt a blast of air as her wings narrowly missed his head. But since all the action was going on behind him, he was mystified as to what was happening. Friedrich jumped up, barking.

"What's the meaning of this!" King Leopold shouted. Horst appeared beside him. There were scratches on his face. King Leopold was suddenly in shadow again before Kol folded her wings back.

Of course. The savage woman. It had always been just a matter of time.

"This is an outrage!" he screamed, as Kol's shrieks echoed away. "You are amongst civilised people now—compose yourself! If I were King I'd have you horse-whipped!"

Friedrich jumped down from his lap and ran to the Winged Woman. She scooped him up. He had a calming influence.

"He betrayed Ursula," she said, fury still evident in her tone.

King Leopold raised his eyebrows. So Horst had done his duty after all. The man had said nothing of it, although his manner, his striding up and down in that annoying way, had shown that something was on his mind.

Horst held a handkerchief to his cheek. "What else did you expect?" he said. "You arrive here unannounced. Uninvited. You throw our lives into chaos!"

King Leopold raised his eyebrows again.

"What if everyone who saw you was to

want their own pair of wings? Where would we be? How would the Republic function?"

"Your life hasn't changed a jot since I arrived," said Kol angrily. "The only person who's been affected is Ursula."

King Leopold interjected, but in a more kindly manner, since Friedrich was evidently so happy in the Winged Woman's arms.

"You must see," he said, "that we cannot have... people... of any kind, just arriving and living here. Things must be done in the proper way."

"I arrived by chance! I would never have landed here by choice. Why would I want to stay? In this grey country with grey people? The air here is polluted—with suspicion and dread and unhappiness. I can't wait to leave!"

"I did my duty as a citizen of the Republic that you insult so easily," said Horst pompously. "And if I had not, someone else would have. The result would be the same. The authorities are involved—as they should be. And your behaviour today is feral. The sooner the authorities arrive, the better."

Of course. It was only a matter of time before the ominous sounding authorities appeared. Ursula's response to this certainty—and what would follow—put Kol in no doubt as to the danger she was in. Arguing with Horst was just wasting precious time. And he was right; someone would have reported her. It didn't matter who.

What or who the authorities were was something Kol had tried to find out, but no one would talk about them. She imagined a great, dark beast that would appear and swallow her.

And when it spat her out she would be wingless.

Ursula was almost immobile with anxiety. Haste was required, of course, but every muscle was frozen with fear and worry. If Kol had not opened the apartment door, Ursula might have stayed standing in her kitchen forever.

"What are you doing here? You're supposed to be in hiding. It's not safe."

"We can't afford to wait," said Kol. "The authorities will be here for me at any time. It's not enough to hide me away. We must leave immediately, for both our sakes."

Ursula shook her head. "Gerhard said the transport cannot come for a week."

She paused. She knew what she had to say, but the words would be like knives to her heart.

Horst opened his door cautiously. He had been under attack ever since he had reported the Winged Woman. Word had spread; some of the tenants had nodded approval but others were distinctly hostile to his act of loyalty to the Republic. Ilse had pelted him with scraps of food when he had passed her door. Her behaviour was ordinarily eccentric but this attack was blatantly rebellious.

And where *were* the authorities? It had been more than twenty-four hours since he had been to the small building in the town centre to make his report. It was baffling, as well as outrageous, that no one from the authorities had yet arrived. Did they not recognise the urgency of the situation? And now here was Hildegard. Since her attitude was quietly subversive at the best of time—

despite her attempts to appear loyal—Horst knew that she would be critical of what he had done.

They stared at one another.

"Aren't you going to invite me in?" asked Hildegard crossly. "But I forgot—you treat your neighbours with contempt. Never mind. I'll say what needs saying here."

Before Horst could stop her she launched into her attack.

"What have you done? You have broken Ursula's heart, that's what! Such betrayal!"

"I acted for the good of all of us," said Horst. Anger was beginning to rise in him. "What's wrong with you people? We have a way of life to defend, a principle."

"To Hell with your principles!" announced Hildegard. "We are talking about real people, people who feel, who hurt, who love. Yes—love! Ursula and Kol love each other!"

There. It had slipped out so easily, this secret that she wasn't sure even the women concerned knew.

Horst's cheeks puffed out in horror. As if this situation could become any worse!

"Well... perhaps I should report Ursula to the authorities as well, then," he spluttered and shut his door smartly.

He leaned against it in the safety of his apartment, his stomach turning over in a mixture of emotion. And on the other side was Hildegard, fuming and trying to swallow her sadness.

They stood at the edge of the Jungfernsee.

"It's wrong for me to go and leave you to the authorities," said Kol. "I cannot help you from the mountains."

"It's too dangerous for you to be here," said Ursula. "I can tell the authorities any number of stories, I can weave a thousand scenarios. They'll find it hard to believe you could exist; it won't be difficult to make you impossible to them."

Each wanted not to cry. Each failed.

"We know where and when we're going to meet," said Ursula. "So this is *au revoir*." She was not going to say that other word.

Kol kissed her. Now was not the time to worry if anyone was watching. Ursula closed her eyes and felt her wings beat behind her, lifting her up into the air. She felt the wing muscles working, the huge effort it demanded, the relationship between each feather and the air.

When she opened her eyes, she had no wings and was gripped by sadness again.

"Tell me to stay," whispered Kol.

"I can't risk them getting you," Ursula whispered back. But it was too much.

"Stay... " she began, but Kol was in the air and slipped out of her embrace.

The Winged Woman flew. She was built for this, Ursula could see that now. She belonged in the air, was graceful in it. Ursula looked at the rising figure and thought, simply, for the first time; *This is the woman I love.*

And then Kol jerked in the air. She was away from the edge of the lake, aware that whatever it was that had caused her to crash into the water might still be hanging over it. Her wings fought for control. Had the bones not healed properly in her damaged wing?

Or was gravity, the pull of the Earth,

simply too strong?

Either way, Kol lost the fight and fell back down again. And this time there was no water to break her fall. Her wings suddenly useless, she fell, upside down and landed on her head.

And was clearly... unbearably...

"Dead," said the old woman, her taste for beer now gone.

The inn was silent.

"At first I thought to bury her by the lake, on the beach where I first saw her." Ursula's voice was almost too quiet to hear. The drinkers strained their ears. "I wanted her nearby. I wanted to make sure the authorities didn't take her. But I knew she'd want to rest in the mountains. So the next week I took her in the van that kind Gerhard had arranged, to the West. I journeyed with the coffin to the mountains, the places she had told me about. It took two weeks to find her people. Two weeks of climbing, of helping the pony drag the cart with my Kol in it, of screaming, weeping, crawling across the ground when grief made me unable to walk.

"Kol had described in great detail where she had lived. She drew maps, although I had destroyed them for fear they'd get into the hands of the authorities. But I had committed them to memory. I found the place, her family.

"It was not the way I wanted to meet them."

The inn remained silent. For some minutes Ursula was unable to continue.

"Her family generously asked me to stay on after Kol's funeral. And I did try. But I found that I couldn't stay still. Grief made me heavy. It was pulling me down.

"So I began to walk. It was the only way to stop the pain from killing me. Grief is like being crushed between two giant stones. So I walked. I feared what would happen if I stopped. I walked down the mountain and back into Germany. It didn't matter where I went, as long as I kept walking. I walked east into Poland. People were kind. Mostly. They could see that I had experienced something that was beyond endurance, although they didn't know what it was. I couldn't tell anyone, you see. I couldn't say the words. I didn't speak Kol's name for fifteen years, not out loud. But, in my head and in my heart, her name was all I heard.

"Not everyone was kind. I have been attacked, robbed. Twice men have forced themselves on me. But I had to keep walking. I have seen every inch of Poland, I think. And West Germany and Switzerland. Perhaps I crossed the border into France. I don't know. It didn't matter. The only place I wouldn't go to was the German Democratic Republic, even after the Wall came down. That country had caused the death of my Kol."

One of the drinkers spoke at last. "And you have been walking for *all these years*? Since I was two years old!"

Ursula looked around her, suddenly aware of the here and now. The landlord was sitting opposite her.

"Would Kol have wanted you to spend your life doing this? She'd want you to be safe. Happy," he said.

"You haven't understood a word I've said,

have you?" said Ursula. "This isn't a choice. I miss her now as much as I did when I saw that she was dead. Happiness is impossible!"

Ursula fell silent and drank her beer. One by one the drinkers drained their glasses and quietly left.

"Your room's ready," said the landlord. "Number 3. You should be comfortable in there. Breakfast is at 8. You've earned that as well, my dear."

Ursula gave him the ghost of a smile. "This is the first time I've told the complete story," she said. "I don't think I'll tell it again, but it's done me good. Thank you. You're a gentleman." She reached into her pocket and took out a feather. It was pristine, a marked contrast to the old woman and her clothing. "This was one of Kol's. I want you to have it."

"Thank you, Ursula," said the landlord, genuinely touched. "I've never heard such a tale. None of us have."

The old woman made her way up the stairs.

The young barmaid, was collecting glasses. "What an odd woman. You don't believe her story, do you?"

The landlord shrugged. "I'm old enough to have seen a few odd things in my life. I think it might be true. She's clearly been on the road for years. Stranger things have happened, I'm sure."

Rachel shrugged. "I think she's just mad," she whispered.

The landlord smiled. But he knew she was wrong.

~

And in the morning, when 8 o'clock came and

went without any sign of Ursula, it was the landlord who knocked politely on the door of Room 3. He opened the door, expecting to find her gone, continuing her obsessive walking, but to his surprise and sadness she was still there.

"You stopped too long, didn't you, Ursula?" he murmured.

The blankets had been thrown to the floor, as if they had offered too much comfort for his guest. All that remained of Ursula was a human-shaped pile of dust, a three-dimensional shadow. Perhaps it was the stopping, the weight of her grief that had killed her, or perhaps the telling of her tale had made it impossible to continue to live. She must have died while stretching, he decided, enjoying the size of the bed, for, reduced to dust, it looked to him as if she had a pair of wings, outstretched and ready to fly.

A lifelong horror, supernatural and Fortean obsessive, Julie Travis began writing fiction in the early 1990s. Her transgenre/slipstream short stories and novellas have been published in the independent press in the United States, Canada and Britain over the past quarter of a century. This is her second short story collection; the first was a single author issue of Storylandia (#15, Wapshott Press, 2015). Born in London in 1967, Julie now lives by the sea in West Cornwall. Find her at www.julietravis.wordpress.com.

The Wapshott Press wishes to thank our sponsors, supporters, and Friends of the Wapshott Press.

Muna Deriane

Kathleen Warner

Rachel Livingston

James and Rebecca White

Jennifer Bentson

Debbie Jones

Steven Acker

Ann Siemens

Suzanne Siegel

Aubrey Hicks

Carol Colin

Ted Waltz

Kathleen Bonagofsky

Cynthia Henderson

Nancy Lilly

Jeff Morawetz

Patricia Nerad

Amanda Nerad

Elaine Padilla

Laurel Sutton

Deana Swart

The Wapshott Press is a 501(c)(3) not-for-profit enterprise publishing work by emerging and established authors and artists. We publish books that should be published. We are very grateful to the people who believe in our plans and goals, as well as our hopes and dreams. Our new website is at www.WapshottPress.org and donations gratefully accepted at www.WapshottPress.net

Printed in Great Britain
by Amazon

82419477R00153